Drawing
from
Memory

Ronnie Berman

Cover Design by Elliot Kreloff
Author photograph by Robert Maslen
Book Design by QA Productions

Send inquiries to Ronnie Berman at ronnieberman@sbcglobal.net

In loving memory of Zoe Graves.

Author Notes

I was inspired to write this book when I first learned about an actual German organization called Action Reconciliation Service for Peace (ARSP), which sends volunteers all over the world. These volunteers, the grandchildren and great-grandchildren of Germans who created the Nazi death camps, support and work with people in social facilities and with survivors of the Holocaust out of a commitment to atone and take responsibility for their nation's past. I was amazed to learn that an organization like this was doing such important work in relative obscurity.

Since its founding in 1958 by the Protestant Church, Action Reconciliation has expanded its services to include challenging right-wing extremism and anti-Semitism, as well as lobbying for the recognition of the victims of Nazi oppression.

In New York, Project Ezra accepts ASRP volunteers to work with the elderly of the Jewish community on the Lower East Side, some of which are Holocaust survivors, and also motivated me to write my novel.

Acknowledgements

To Zoe Graves who first told me about Action Reconciliations' existence.

I am grateful to Linda Palmer who encouraged and guided me in turning my story into a novel, Eduardo Santiago who nurtured me through the final draft of my novel, encouraging me to deepen and expand my story, and Diana Wagman for being an extra pair of eyes and motivating me to heighten my story.

I would like to thank Kate Robbins, Suzanne Lyons and Ellen Krass for always believing in *Drawing From Memory*.

I want to thank my brother, Bruce Berman and my sister-in-law, Suzanne, for always being supportive and cheering me on from the sidelines.

I would like to thank William Bentrim for his kindness, reassurance and helpfulness.

I want to thank Catherine Marciniak for her expertise in story telling and editing.

I want to thank my wonderful husband, Robert Maslen for his love, unending support and for providing the author photograph for this book.

I want to thank Elliot Kreloff for his much appreciated perfect cover design.

I would like to thank Arleen Jacobius for her friendship, support, help and encouragement.

Out of suffering have emerged the strongest souls;
the most massive characters are seared with scars.

Kahlil Gibran

Chapter 1

Verdammt! Kurt Lichter cursed under his breath as he cautiously steered his battered 1978 Volkswagen convertible around one of the Autobahn's most dangerous curves. He almost lost control of the wheel, fighting the hot August wind to keep his long blond hair from blowing into his eyes. A Gothic cross hanging from his left ear floated in mid-air. He barely made out the sign announcing the Berlin-Tegel Airport exit as he drove under it.

Cars whizzed by, but he wanted everything to slow down. He glanced over at Karin, sitting so close to him; her hip bumped against his to the beat of the heavy metal tune on the radio. He wanted nothing more than to turn around, go back to her apartment, crawl into bed and hold her tight forever. He wasn't prepared for life in Berlin without her.

She seemed oblivious to his whispered ramblings, his vile mood, wearing tight black designer jeans with a black tee shirt, the same outfit as Kurt, only his jeans were from a thrift shop in Kreuzberg, while hers were from the trendiest shop in Berlin. Nonetheless, they were often mistaken for twins. Both were tall and lean, had long straight blonde hair, light blue eyes with a gray tinge and chiseled, striking features, most notably their lower lips, which naturally turned downward, making Karin appear mysterious and alluring, while Kurt's evoked irritable, churlish disdain.

Karin leaned forward and turned up the volume on the radio to an almost deafening level.

What does she fucking care? he thought. In five hours she'll be in New York studying film, while I'm left all alone in Berlin studying my own grief, my own useless fucked up life.

"Christ, can't we go any faster? We have to be there at least two hours in advance to get through security," Karin said, shoving her watch in his face.

He wished they'd miss the plane. It would delay his pain for a few more hours and, if he was lucky, maybe another day.

"Don't worry, you're not going to miss the goddamn plane," he shouted above the music and the wind, now pushing the old VW Bug to its maximum speed against his better judgment. The fastest he ever took it was seventy kilometers per hour when the engine had growled, sparked, spewed black smoke and smelled like burnt rubber. This time the Bug rumbled as if it ate something that didn't agree with it.

Karin smacked his arm. "Get me there in one piece, if you don't mind. What's your problem?"

He turned down the radio. "You're my problem. What the fuck am I going to do without you?" He shouted, then, his voice softening he added, "You're the only thing in my life that matters."

"Don't say that. It's not true." She gently caressed his arm. "Start painting again."

"I can't anymore. You know that," he said, removing her hand abruptly. He knew she was right, but hadn't the energy or inclination. Painting was now a part of his past, something he was formerly obsessed with and now wasn't, like a food that you once couldn't get enough of, but now just the smell of it made you gag.

In spite of its age and condition, the car, as if responding to Karin's deepest desires, lurched and accelerated, almost missing the airport exit. Kurt veered into the right-hand lane, barely avoiding a shiny, black Mercedes as his rear view mirror was partially blocked by Karin's luggage in the back seat. The driver pounded on his horn. Kurt shot him the finger.

"*Arschloch!*"

Kurt drove into the airport's temporary parking lot and found a space in the back, while Karin brushed her hair.

"I thought you were in a hurry," he said, stepping out of the car and opening the trunk.

"I look like I was caught in a wind tunnel," she said, checking herself in the rear-view mirror. Kurt watched her and again rejected a thought that had come to him frequently in regards to her: that she was a poseur.

As long as he'd known her, Karin never missed an opportunity to gaze admirably at her own reflection in any available mirror or any pane of glass.

She got out of the car, grabbed her carry-on canvas bag out of the trunk, flung the bag's long strap over her shoulder and walked briskly ahead of him toward the terminal.

Kurt hauled her two large wheelies out of the back seat and dragged them, lagging behind, hating every step forward. He watched her sprint through the automatic doors. This was the best day of her life and his worst. After all their years together, battling adolescence, their parents, professing their undying love to each other. Now she was happily off to NYU Film School, which happened to be the alma mater of her favorite filmmaker, Martin Scorsese, and unhappily for him, over six thousand kilometers away.

For some reason, which he could never figure out, Karin adored Scorsese's filmmaking style. She would go on and on about his creative use of violence and profanity—depicting the raw, gritty, underbelly of life, which she didn't know a rat's ass about. He always thought that her obsession with Scorsese was a way of making her appear more complex than she actually was.

Karin never discussed her decision with him, probably knowing he would do his best to talk her out of it. He knew she applied, but also knew that it was very prestigious, difficult to get into, and so he didn't take it that seriously. When she told him the good news, he was devastated. His future choices were fewer and a lot less fun. He had turned twenty-one last Tuesday and had his parents breathing down his neck about getting a real job, a job with a pension and security. They'd been tormenting him lately with continuous threats that if he didn't stop wasting his life away and start taking his future seriously, they were going to throw him and his belongings out of their house. He would have to fend for himself.

He knew deep down he'd be better off out of their house. His parents' contemptuous stares greeted him every morning and their barely audible "*Guten Nacht*," every night before they went to sleep, were grim reminders of how bitter his relationship with them had become. He had absolutely nothing in common with them. They didn't understand him and he had no idea what made them tick. There was no common ground.

But, was he ready to face the world by himself? Karin had been his anchor grounding his feet on this earth, preventing him from drifting off into oblivion. She led and he followed, willingly avoiding making any serious decisions for himself. He wasn't sure what would become of him without her.

The doors to the Lufthansa terminal reluctantly slid open for him.

He surveyed the crowds and spotted Karin in the back of the check-in line aiming her iPhone randomly at the hordes of people inside. Kurt called out to her, and she waved him forward, focusing her phone on him as he angled his way through the maze of barriers to the back of the line and stood next to her. She brought it right up to his face. "Stop," he said, pushing it away as an announcement came over the loudspeaker broadcasting her flight.

"You're actually leaving? I still can't believe it," he said, wrapping his arms around her tightly.

"Aren't you happy for me? You know how much I've wanted this," she said, pulling away. Her lower lip folded over for that petulant look he always was a sucker for.

"Yes, yes . . . of course I'm happy for you . . . I'm so sorry," he said quickly, but didn't mean it. He knew he was acting like a child: selfish and insensitive. So be it. That's who he was right now.

"Come to New York," she said.

"Sure, tell your rich father to pay for both of us."

"He's not that rich . . . or that generous. Have you thought about that peace group? They send people all over the world, even New York. I think it's your best chance—maybe your only chance."

"What group?" he said, knowing exactly what she was talking about, but not wanting to argue about it again. She had brought it up several times when they talked about his options.

"You know. We've talked about it before." She didn't bother disguising her irritation with him.

"Like I really give a shit about what happened over seventy years ago," he said.

"You think I do, but it can get you to New York to be with me."

After she checked in, they hurriedly followed the signs to her gate and silently hopped on a crowded escalator. He deliberated joining that organization, knowing she had a point, but it seemed like such a long shot.

"Look at me. You think they would really take someone like me?" he said, turning her around to face him.

"They take all sorts of people and they need volunteers, especially now that the draft has been eliminated," Karin said, grabbing his hand firmly. "You're a very clever boy and can figure out a way if you really want to."

They rushed to the security checkpoint line. He would have to leave her there. His heart hurt. He pulled her into a long and turbulent last kiss, almost swallowing her, drawing the attention of everyone around them.

She unlocked herself from his embrace, pulled down her tee shirt and stroked his hair back from his forehead.

"Just look at their website. At least do that," she said, smiling sympathetically. He didn't want sympathy; he wanted tears and indecision. He wanted her to stay.

"I'll call you when I get there." She said it the way people talk when they're just going across town. It wasn't cold or dry, but it wasn't warm either. It was practical. Karin had always been a very practical girl.

He nodded and walked away.

Chapter 2

Kurt wandered aimlessly down stylish, spotless, Kurfuerstendamn Boulevard, repulsed by the throngs of tourists and affluent Berliners, sidewalks lined with chain stores, souvenir shops, restaurants and cafes, and worst of all an old McDonald's and a new Starbucks. He hated these monuments to globalization.

Carrying a frayed, black canvas bag over one shoulder, he removed his leather jacket and slung it over his other arm. He could feel beads of perspiration forming on the back of his neck. It was unseasonably warm for the end of September, even the leaves on the trees were still green.

It had been a month since Karin left, but it seemed much longer. Her phone calls and emails reminded him how far away she was and made him miss her more than he thought possible. All he wanted was to have her with him, to touch her, to hold her, make love to her. Nothing else interested him.

He started out each day charged with the task of finding a job to appease his parents, but today he didn't have the heart for it. He'd filled out dozens of applications for retail chain stores, cafés, restaurants weeks ago and had not heard back from any of them. There were simply no real jobs for someone without any marketable skills.

He passed the Amedia Hotel where he and Karin would visit the art gallery in the lobby whenever there was a new showing. They'd talk about how one day he would have his paintings there. Stupid dreams.

He spotted a man wearing a black beret with salt and pepper frizzy hair, drawing a caricature of a young Asian woman in front of a small café next to the hotel. Her large family crowded around the artist, hovering over him as he sketched. They laughed hysterically at the finished product.

Kurt considered doing something like that, but how many exaggerated cartoons would you have to produce in a day to make it worthwhile? It would be too demoralizing for him to do anything like that, particularly since he had stopped painting.

He sauntered by Karstadt's Department Store, Karin's favorite place to shop, and remembered how she'd spend hours trying on clothes. Sometimes he sneaked into her fitting room and they'd silently make love, their orgasms intensified by the fear of getting caught.

He reached *Fasenenstrasse*; the aroma of cinnamon and apples emanating from the Wintergarten Café beckoned him to stop. Another attraction of the café was that they had WIFI. The noisy room was packed. All of the small laminated wood tables and wrought iron chairs were taken with people of all ages glued to their laptops and tablets.

He stepped up to the counter and ordered an apple strudel and a café Americain from a girl who looked like she was twelve. She stared at him contemptuously when she handed him his coffee and strudel on a small cardboard tray. He flashed her a great big smile. Usually, Europeans ordered cappuccinos or espressos. He couldn't care less about what she thought.

Karin had started ordering American coffee once she was accepted to NYU so she'd be in sync with everybody else in New York. He had gotten into the habit of requesting the same just to be in sync with her.

He headed out to the outdoor terrace that housed small, white, round, plastic patio tables with large yellow umbrellas sprouting out of the middle. A hot breeze perfumed the air with intoxicating, sugary sweet smells mixed with the strong, bitter scent of roasted coffee beans. He found an empty table in back, sat down, opened his shoulder bag, retrieved Karin's hand-me-down laptop. Then he flipped open the lid plastered with Metallica, Black Sabbath and Ramones stickers and fired it up. It was a few years old and took several minutes to power on. He knew she'd be at her computer as they'd prearranged this meeting.

He clicked on instant messaging and viewed Karin's last message. She wanted to know if he'd heard anything back from the peace group? He'd sent out his application a couple of weeks ago, actually his "by proxy" application, since she basically filled it out for him and obtained the two required references.

Kurt was particularly uncomfortable with the way she exaggerated his relationship with his grandfather since she knew that some assignments involved working with the elderly. She had also touted his artistic abilities and that he was always willing to volunteer his services to his community. A load of crap. He couldn't believe that she looked up his old high school art teacher and pestered her Uncle Anton, a prominent philanthropist in Berlin, to give him glowing references. He had helped her uncle design pamphlets and flyers for his charity events many times over the years, but they hadn't talked in a while.

He rapidly hammered in his reply. *Nothing yet, but the minute I hear I will let you know. It has been only two and a half weeks. Be patient.* Karin answered instantaneously that she understood. She just was anxious to see him and wanted to make sure he was keeping an eye out for it. Nothing wrong with that, he thought. They typed in their goodbyes, he powered off, closed the lid and bit off a healthy chunk of his strudel. As he licked his lips, savoring the rich cinnamon flavor, a dark looming presence blocked the sunlight surrounding his table. The shadows had voices that he hadn't heard for a long time—voices he hoped he would never hear again.

"Hey, Lichter, get into any good fights lately?" said one voice, low and mocking.

"Still painting your nightmares?" said another, this one nasally, as if the speaker was trying to hold back a runny nose.

Kurt looked up at two young men hovering over his table.

Oh fuck, it's Schumacher and Konig. Where the hell did they come from?

During his tumultuous two years at the Berlin Arts University, they would call him Salvador Dillydally because his paintings were surrealistic and he would spend an inordinate amount of time on each one. That got to be his nickname among the other students, whose painting styles were either abstract or representational. Sometimes he got so irritated, he'd answer their taunts with his fists.

Kurt stiffened. "*Fick dich, Arschloch,*" he said and shot them the finger. They leisurely walked away. Their laughter echoed in his ears as he finished his coffee. He would have punched them out, but thought better of it. The last thing he needed now was trouble with those two assholes.

He tossed his unfinished pastry and proceeded toward Kurfuerstendamn station. It was time to head home after another unproductive day in the city. His twenties were supposed to be his glory years; that was what everyone always had told him, but for him it seemed like these were going to be his shit years. They had clearly misinformed him.

Kurt trudged down *Dorfstrasse* to the small faded red brick two-story row house in Lichtenberg he shared with his family. He hated the look of those houses, so working-class—all of them mirror images of the other. The only difference might be the color of the curtains that adorned the thin rotted wood framed windows or the flowers in the window boxes. He despised the red gingham curtains his mother put up and her red plastic roses. Was it too much for her to take care of real flowers? He opened the front door that once was white but was now grayed with age and covered with handprints. His father had promised to repaint it years ago.

He sneaked up the stairs. The last thing he wanted was to see anybody. The setting sun illuminated his closet-sized room, casting orange-pinkish shadows on his worn furniture and clutter, making the space appear larger and more interesting than it actually was. He gazed at his paintings covering the walls—wounded soldiers with abnormally large heads holding up peace signs splattered with blood. The Madonna holding a cross, with her bruised baby nailed to it. Hordes of monks dressed in blood-stained brown robes carrying melting steel-gray rifles.

He labored over each of these paintings for months, only to have his teachers and fellow students call them his nightmares. To him they were surreal representations of the violence and hypocrisy in the world around him. They just didn't get it.

He glanced at photographs of Karin at various ages, which he planted all over his room: on top of the bureau, night table, the portable television and a small table that served as a desk. Each photograph brought back a specific happy memory. He stared at a small picture of him and Karin kissing passionately, arms tightly woven around each other, tongues intertwined. It was taken in one of those curtained photo booths in Europa Center, Karen's favorite mall, and was clipped to the top of his high school graduation picture encased in a black metal frame. He'd snipped it from the other pictures in the strip as it was his favorite.

Kurt dropped down on his bed, removed his laptop from his bag, powered it up, flipped the lid, clicked on a link and watched Karin posing playfully in the nude. He was immediately mesmerized. Loud persistent knocking jolted Kurt from his deep trance.

"What do you want, Mutti?"

The door swung open with a groan. His mother eyed the video of Karin as Kurt scrambled to quickly click it off and back onto his screensaver, a stunning picture of Karin in front of the Brandenburg Gate.

Kurt looked up at his mother's large frame covered with a faded flowered house dress, like the one she wore when he was a child, and sighed. She'd always had on shabby slippers, but now there was the added attraction of her swollen and purple ankles.

Why did she never make an effort to look like anything more than a defeated hausfrau?

She stared at him with disdain. "So this is what you call looking for work like you promised? You think that girl still cares about you?" she said, glaring at his screen.

"What do you know about it?" he said, knowing that his mother only saw the rich, overindulged side of Karin and nothing else.

"I know what a mother knows. I know you'd do anything for her, and that girl has never done anything for you, except give you trouble. You're such a fool."

His mother had always been ill-tempered. She'd wake him every morning for school with all the warmth of a prison guard.

"You waste your time on this," she said and plopped a business sized envelope on top of a pile of papers on his desk. She tapped a fat finger on Project Remembrance's return address. "This has nothing to do with you . . . when your father can get you a good job."

"Being a postman? Why can't you just leave me alone?"

"You're my only child and no matter what you think about me, I still worry about you."

There was no denying he was her child. Their resemblance was unmistakable. Their disgruntled frowns were identical. His mother slammed the door as she left. Kurt tripped over a pile of books and magazines to retrieve the envelope. He paused before he tore it open. He removed a letter and a brochure. He unfolded the letter, smoothing in out with his palm, and read it. They were granting him an interview next week. That was quick. Why so soon?

He grasped the brochure and read the title: Project Remembrance—Pathway to Peace. He slid into his chair and turned to the first page.

Project Remembrance is a volunteer corps, consisting of the offspring of Germans who created the Nazi extermination camps. When Germans slaughtered millions of Jews and other undesirables, there were those of us who did not want this annihilation, but did nothing to prohibit it. We Germans will never be at peace with ourselves. So we send our volunteers to work all over the world. By serving in the present all the people who suffered in the past, we accept the responsibility to atone for Germany's atrocious crimes.

Kurt reread that paragraph several times. Was he ready to accept responsibility for what happened back then? He studied all this in school and at that time, he felt disgust for his country's actions, but he, like most of his classmates, was ambivalent and defensive. It was horrible, yes, but it was a long time ago and certainly not his fault. Will the rest of the fucking world ever let him forget? Why was his generation still being forced to carry the infinite burden of their grandparents and great-grandparents' war crimes on their backs like pack mules?

And what about America and the genocide of Native Americans and the brutal treatment of blacks brought to their country as slaves? What about England, France, Italy and Spain, which massacred countless numbers of indigenous people in their imperial quests all over the planet? Why were Germans singled out as the world's worst villains?

He dropped the brochure on his desk and crashed back on his bed, fired up his computer, clicked on the link of Karin naked, and decided that she was really worth it. He would do anything to be with her again.

Chapter 3

He had lost track of time a while ago. It was either very late or early the next day. Kurt stumbled in and out of Berlin's sleaziest dives, fulfilling his goal to become as hammered as possible. He desperately needed to decompress after spending days in front of his dresser mirror reciting Karin's answers to the questions on his application, practicing different vocal inflections and facial expressions like an actor rehearsing for opening night.

The pressure of preparing for the interview was unbearable. He'd never been good at selling himself. He would trip over his tongue, stammering his responses, and if that wasn't bad enough, beads of perspiration would form on his forehead and drip down his face. He was fully aware of his proclivity for fucking up pretty much everything in his life that mattered to him. This time he couldn't afford to do that. He had to ace this interview.

His head was gummy from the joint he shared with a couple of guys in front of the last club he wandered into. He approached Die Roht Bar, drawn to it by its bright red façade. Deafening loud techno music spilled out onto the street. He staggered in, weaving his way past a husky security guard with a shaved head and a lengthy dirty blond, braided goatee, who was busy checking the IDs of a group of boys who clearly looked like they were under the legal drinking age.

Multi-colored strobe lights flashed over the crowd. Kurt squinted as he surveyed the scene. He knew no one there and no one knew him. He tried to remember if this was the sixth or seventh place he'd wandered into tonight, but couldn't.

The dance floor was packed with people wearing neon hair extensions and leather surgical masks. The dancers were dressed in black and several barely clothed women slithered up and down stripper poles like snakes on trees. The crowd gyrated as one under the flickering colored lights to the throbbing techno music.

Kurt danced alone, waving his arms like a large wounded bird, twisting his hips, sliding his feet along the floor as if he were ice skating, almost losing his balance. The nearly naked woman who joined him swayed her hips, more a dare than an invitation. Kurt grinned at her, taking in her shockingly pink hair as he tried to mirror her moves but couldn't quite get it. She laughed at his attempt. Another woman, wearing a skin-tight black sheer mini dress, with long platinum blonde hair that reached her thighs, slid down one of the poles and joined them. Kurt couldn't believe his good luck.

He took the dare and shimmied his hips toward the blonde, gazing at her with heavy-lidded eyes, and then twisted in the direction of the pink-haired woman, lowering his head close to her bosom as if he was going to rest it there. The blonde pushed the pink-haired woman into another dancer so she could have Kurt all to herself.

"Who the fuck do you think you're shoving, bitch?" the pink-haired woman shouted.

"Back off, slut. You don't own him." The blonde swung and the pink-haired dancer struck back.

He tried to pry them apart, but the two women ganged up on him, punching him all over.

Two enormous bouncers with eager fists grabbed Kurt by the arm, separating him from the blur of pink and platinum, and pulled him toward the exit. He swung wildly at one of the bouncers, who with one blow knocked him onto the pavement.

The glaring sun blazed through his naked window. The white, pull-down shade was rolled all the way to the top. He must have been too drunk to pull it down the night before.

He drifted into a dreadful memory of last night's debacle. He remembered two supersized men grabbing him, throwing him out of a red door, where he landed on his ass like some washed up *trinker*.

He could barely lift his head. With great difficulty, he managed to swing his legs over the edge and brace himself on the bed. His muscles were sore and his head ached. Once on his feet, he looked over at his desk and saw the letter from Project Remembrance. His appointment was today. *Jesus Christ!* Why the fuck did he feel compelled to get so loaded that he ended up looking as if he went twelve rounds with Mike Tyson?

He checked himself in the mirror above his dresser. He had bruises on his cheeks and forehead. He opened his closet and took out his one suit, black gabardine, and laid it on his bed. The last time he wore it was for his maternal grandmother's funeral in Munich. His family had stood around the grave stiff as soldiers with emotionless faces. A year ago, a scorching hot day that made him sweat so heavily, he was soaking wet by the time they lowered the casket into the ground.

He grabbed the jacket and sniffed under each sleeve. It still reeked. He snatched a bottle of Calvin Klein's Eternity, a present from Karin last Christmas, and generously sprayed each underarm. He smelled it again and the body odor was replaced with the tangy scent of a

Lutzowplatz prostitute. He figured once he was outside in the fresh air the pungent aroma would be neutralized.

He picked up a picture of Karin. *I hope you appreciate this.*

He removed his earring, slicked his hair back and snuck into the one bathroom in his house and scrounged around in his mother's drawer in the cabinet under the sink. He fished out an old tube of cover-up left over from the days when she wore makeup. It was oily with age, but usable. He applied it on his bruises and it seemed to do the trick.

Kurt strolled casually into the large, bright kitchen, grinning, foreseeing the shock value of his appearance. His father sat in his postman's uniform at a rectangular table covered with a yellow plastic tablecloth, his big pot belly protruding over his trousers. As always, deeply engrossed in his newspaper, he ate his burnt toast silently. A 55-year-old man devoid of any human emotion except anger. Kurt had no memory of ever receiving any kindness or affection from him after his sixth birthday. His father was furious with him for doing something at the party, something Kurt for the life of him couldn't remember. After that, the only contact he had with his father during his entire childhood was at the receiving end of a leather belt strap.

Next to his father, condemned to a wheelchair where he would spend the rest of his days, was his paternal grandfather, who had been living with his family since Kurt was a baby. Kurt would occasionally help his parents care for him: administering his medicines, bathing him and making his bed. Kurt was about to greet his grandfather, but the empty eyes and permanent snarl, and the way he hunched over the table and sipped steaming hot coffee out of a large mug stopped him. For his grandfather some days were better than others, and this was clearly not a good one.

Kurt knew little of his grandfather's past. He had always

vehemently refused to talk about his war years. It was *verboten* to even bring up the war in the Lichter household if his grandfather was in, or for that matter, out of the room. The only sounds his grandfather uttered were his periodic screams during his sleep. Kurt often wondered if his grandfather ever remembered those terrifying dreams when he woke up and if those nightmares were spurred by the crimes he either witnessed or committed during the war.

Kurt's mother was at her old, claw footed, gas stove violently scrambling eggs. The offensive smell permeated the air. She had on the same white apron covered with food stains over the same cotton flowered house dress that she'd worn yesterday and the day before. The last time he saw his mother crack a smile was when he was accepted into the Berlin University of the Arts. He knew she cared about him, but her constant hounding irritated him beyond belief. Maybe that was a mother's job—and if it was, she had reached the height of her profession. She would die an accomplished woman.

A warm breeze fluttered the checkered curtains on the kitchen window making the only sound in the room. Mornings, his father often said, were not for conversation. Kurt imagined each of them in their own stratosphere, orbiting their own separate planet. It was like living with a group of androids—they appeared to be humans, but there was no real visual evidence that they were; their setting was always on automatic pilot.

Startled by Kurt's well-groomed appearance, his mother turned and froze with her scrambling fork held mid-air. His father looked up from his paper. "Where are you going dressed like that?" he said.

"To that Holocaust group so he can be with his *reich schlampe*, yes?" his mother said, dishing out overcooked scrambled eggs onto his father and grandfather's plates.

"We pay them reparations—money every month that comes out of my paycheck, what more do they want?" his father said loudly.

His mother went over to her son and gently placed her hand on his arm. "Your father and I weren't even born yet. Why should you care about those things?"

His grandfather gaped at Kurt with a glazed look. "You think we had a choice? You have no idea what happened to people who opposed them," he said, his voice gravelly, almost inaudible, and he instantly wheeled himself out of the room.

Kurt was stunned. He hadn't heard his grandfather speak a complete sentence in years.

Kurt's father rose from the table and stepped in front of him and stood erect, chest puffed out, his feet a foot apart, as if he was about to pounce on him. "I was going to talk to my boss for you. Better yet, you could join the army—it made a man out of me, maybe it would do the same for you. You think you're going to be a great artist someday? Really? You want to waste your life away. Is that what you want?"

He glared at his father. "*Verdammt,* it's my life. I'll do what I please."

"Then do it somewhere else. Not in my house," he bellowed. "You're just a good-for-nothing dreamer. That's what you are. You couldn't even complete art school for Christ sakes."

His father grabbed Kurt's shoulders and shook him. Kurt found himself staring at eyes the same color as his and just as full of pain and confusion.

With a hard shove to his father's chest, Kurt freed himself from his grip. He quickly straightened his suit jacket.

"I'll never be like you," he said walking out, proud to have had the last word, amazed his father didn't punch him in the stomach like he frequently had when Kurt was younger.

*   *   *

Kurt sat in Project Remembrance's hot stuffy outer office on a black vinyl couch that clung to his gabardine pants. He waited to see Hannah Kruger, one of the organization's directors, and was relieved that he would be interviewed by a female. He usually felt at ease with women. He seemed to appeal to them more than he did to men.

He viewed photographs that lined the walls depicting volunteers involved in various activities: rebuilding synagogues, churches, and cemeteries in Western Europe; picking fruit on farms and helping the handicapped in Israel; conducting tours at sites in former concentration camps; and couldn't imagine himself doing any of those things. He never was a Boy Scout and had no intention of being one now.

A door opened and a petite, middle-aged woman walked toward him, introduced herself and shook his hand. She was casually dressed in poorly fitting khakis and an apparently cheap yellow and white V-neck striped knit top, probably from one of those discount clothing stores. Her hair was gray and devoid of any style. She had a deep, bass voice, too big for her small stature.

She seemed like one of those pathetic do-gooders who thought that they were superior because they cared more about the well-being of others than most people.

She ushered him into a small, lackluster office, and asked him to sit in a high-back, uncomfortable metal chair across from her desk. She hurried around and sat down in her faux leather chair and picked up a manila folder, which was next to a pitcher of water and a stack of clear, plastic cups.

"I am so pleased to meet you," she said with an ingratiating smile, revealing a tiny, bright green piece of spinach stuck in the gap between her two front teeth. It was further punctuated by her bright pink lipstick, the only makeup she wore. She opened the folder and removed an application. His initial nervous anticipation of this interview was dissipated by her demeanor. He had expected a *frömmlerisch Ordens-shwester* (pious nun) and it was kind of sad to see how very ordinary she was.

She poured herself a cup of water, offered him one and he accept-ed. The piece of spinach disappeared after a few sips of her water, im-proving her appearance immensely. He was relieved. He didn't know how long he would be able look at her with that repulsive green rem-nant of her lunch facing him.

"I called you in today as an unusual situation has arisen. One of our volunteers working at a senior outreach center in New York City is unable to complete his term for personal reasons. I'd just read your application when I got the news and thought of you," she said and leaned in toward him. "Would you be available to start your term on such short notice?"

Shit, so soon. He was momentarily stunned by the immediacy of his assignment. He hesitated before responding. He was suddenly ambivalent. Yes, he was dying to be with Karin again, but he never thought he would get this far.

"I think I can. I mean, it might be possible," he said, obsessing about all the things he would have to do on such short notice. He would have to sell his car, which no one in their right mind would want as it died a few days after taking Karin to the airport. He'd have to gather up all his belongings and decide what he needed in New York that he didn't already have. He knew he probably would have to ask his parents for the money to buy those things and that surely would cause another big blow-up.

"Okay . . . Tell me something about your relationship with your grandfather and also why you want to help Holocaust survivors?" She stared skeptically at him. He sensed she picked up his uncertainty.

He took another sip of his water before he spoke and decided to tell the absolute truth regardless of the consequences. "To be honest," he said, "I sometimes help my mother take care of my grandfather who is a very unpleasant, broken man. I have no idea what he did during the war, but it had to be really awful from the way he is now. I think he belongs to the 'I was only following orders', 'kill or be killed' group of Germans. We don't have a warm, caring relationship. I try to stay out of his way as much as I can and I'm not so sure I want to help Holocaust survivors. I suspect that they're probably just as miserable as he is."

"Oh, I see," she said.

Kurt gazed at this homely woman and noticed her eyes narrowing and the lines on her forehead becoming more pronounced as if she was sizing him up and didn't like what she saw. He wondered if she could sense that he'd be the last person you would want to help old people. Kindness and compassion never were a part of his nature. He was sure she could perceive that. She probably concluded that his application was packed with lies. A complete fraud.

"I'm glad you're being honest with me. I respect that," she said, leaning toward him. "I actually think you'll greatly benefit from this experience and my gut tells me that you'll be better at it than you think. Why don't you sleep on it and let me know tomorrow morning whether or not you'll be able to accept this assignment. Call before ten," she said, handing him her card. "I'll have to set up an express training course for you before you leave."

He nodded apprehensively. They both stood and she held her hand to him for him to shake and he did. Her handshake was firm, her smile sincere enough, almost too sincere. She seemed to see something in Kurt, but he couldn't imagine what.

Chapter 4

Kurt pressed his face against the window of the Lufthansa jet as it made its descent toward JFK, anxiously surveying the New York City skyline below, gazing at the city he had been so jealous of, the city that stole his Karin. Now here he was, gliding over it, staring at the towering gray monolithic structures that blocked out most of the sky and hid thousands of stars from view.

The anticipation of being with Karin again and starting a new life overwhelmed him. His smiling mouth left an imprint on the window, which made his smile last even longer.

For once in his life, he felt certain that he made the right decision. He would live in New York with everything paid for and a weekly stipend. He'd have to be around old Jews for twelve months, but maybe Hanna Kruger was right. Maybe, it wouldn't be as bad as it sounded, and it might even do him some good.

The plane made a relatively smooth landing. That was a good omen. Kurt watched the passengers pull their carry-ons from the overhead compartments and make their way impatiently toward the front of the plane. He hung back, grabbed his threadbare black shoulder bag from under his seat, slung it over his shoulder, stood and waited for a break in the line. He was just as eager to get off, but not like the herd of cattle ahead of him. At last the aisle cleared. With a rough yank, he removed his own carry-on: an old beat-up black wooden paint box with a skull and crossbones boldly painted in white and silver on both sides. He'd recreated his unfinished wooden paint box his first year at the Arts university, so no one would mistake his box for theirs. It was undeniably unique.

A wave of anxiety engulfed him as he followed the crowd to immigration, a bit nervous about how he would fare. He'd filled out all his forms on the plane as instructed by the overly enthusiastic flight attendant and had all of his documents and the special visa from Project Remembrance inside his laptop shoulder bag, but with his long hair, earring and general scruffy appearance who knows? They might take him for a drug mule. Maybe he shouldn't have worn his standard black heavy metal attire.

He retrieved all his forms and documents from his bag, but when it was his turn, the efficacious Latino agent who had a pencil thin mustache that looked like it was drawn on, barely looked at him. He checked Kurt's papers and waved him through to the customs/baggage area. All his worrying for nothing.

At the baggage carousel, people impatiently hovered over the moving luggage, ready to swoop and retrieve their bags. He snaked his way to the front, surveyed the luggage winding around and easily spotted his big black duffle bag, as it was the only piece with a silver skull painted across the top, to match his paint box.

His anticipation of seeing Karin again peaked. He could hardly breathe. Kurt stepped out a bit, strained his neck toward the area right outside of customs to see if he could spot her waiting for him, but she wasn't there. Sure she helped him get to New York, but he wondered if she still felt the same about him as she had before she left. There would be a lot of other men at NYU—young and hip film students, most likely a lot cooler than he. Was she tempted enough so as to hook up with one of them?

He got through customs easily enough, except for one glitch. With raised eyebrows that almost reached the top of his forehead, the customs agent stared intently at Kurt's paint box. Without one word to Kurt, he put on surgical gloves, opened the box and picked up each cracked, rusting, half-used tube of oil paint, jerked off the caps, held the tubes up to his nose and sniffed them as if he were sampling expensive perfumes. He then twisted the caps back on tightly, placed them back in Kurt's box and proceeded to sift through all of the contents of Kurt's duffel bag and even checked his toothpaste and shaving cream for any suspicious chemicals.

With a disappointed sigh, the agent hurled everything on the counter back into Kurt's duffel bag and waved the next person forward.

Kurt surveyed the crowd and glanced at his watch, it was now 7:00 p.m. She said she would meet him at 6:00. He couldn't believe that Karin would stand him up. His anxiety gave way to anger. He found a spot against a windowed wall next to the exit and sat cross-legged on the floor, his back erect, his head high, as if he was protesting her lateness. What the fuck? What if she got the flight time wrong? What if she got the date wrong? She could be scatterbrained some times. Where the hell was she?

He headed toward a bank of pay phones. Then stopped. He didn't want to seem pathetic. His head felt heavy and he let it hang down, feeling the stretch on his neck.

Someone slipped up behind him and placed hands over his eyes.

"Guess who?"

Annoyed, relieved, excited, he held his position.

"Marty Scorsese?"

He spun around and pulled Karin into a kiss, almost consuming her. His passion was very much alive. After a few seconds he broke away. "Where the hell were you? Fuck . . . I've been waiting here for hours."

"You wouldn't believe it. We had to watch a goddamn Fassbinder film, *Berlin Alexanderplatz!* It was a twelve-hour nightmare," she said with an added tinge of New York-ese to her German accent.

Kurt held her face in his hands and kissed her tenderly and eyed her black leather mini-skirt and a black skin-tight lace shirt.

"I guess you're worth the wait."

She smiled and grabbed his arm. "We'd better hurry if we want to get a cab. The line could be forever."

They were lucky and got a cab in a few seconds. The turbaned cab driver loaded Kurt's stuff into the trunk and asked for their destination in a thick Hindi accent. Kurt thought it strange that a foreigner would be driving a cab but instantly realized that this would be the first of the many disparities he would encounter here.

Karin slipped into the back seat. "Tenth Street between First and Avenue A and please take the Triborough," she said, sounding like she was a seasoned New Yorker.

Kurt slid in next to her. He had no idea where Tenth Street between First and Avenue A was, but it sounded like the most interesting address he had ever heard.

As they drove over the bridge, he took in the nighttime skyline on the other side of the river. He'd seen it many times before in movies and on TV, but seeing it in person was a whole different experience. He felt a surge of excitement he hadn't experienced in a very long time.

Karin ranted on about the virtues of the city that never shuts down while the cab weaved its way from uptown to midtown to downtown. Kurt was mesmerized by the changing neighborhoods every ten blocks or so, from the age and height of the apartment buildings, to the high-end boutiques to discount stores, to the color and ethnicity of the people and the style of clothing they wore. It was like each section was a separate community, almost like little cities, with a unique character of their own and very different from Berlin.

Karin's East Village apartment building was an old six-story, faded brick walk-up. She led the way up the front steps and dug in her handbag, took out her keys, unlocked and opened the door.

Kurt trailed behind her. After five flights of dragging his luggage up the steep steps, Kurt could barely catch his breath.

"How much longer?"

"Just one more floor. Don't worry, you'll get in shape in no time."

She opened the door to a two-room apartment with a kitchen alcove in the first room. The rooms were narrow, the size of large walk-in closets. In the first room, he glanced at Karin's NYU notebooks strewn across a small black wooden dining table with matching chairs, which appeared to serve as a kitchen, dining and living room, with a black vinyl loveseat smacked against one wall and a slim, black laminate rectangular coffee table. Movie posters from several Scorsese films lined the walls.

"It's called a railroad flat, because of how it is laid out," Karen said. "Like a rail car. Pretty cozy, don't you think?"

"It's *gemütlich* all right," Kurt said, gazing at each poster—*Taxi Driver, Goodfellas, Raging Bull, The Aviator* and *The Departed*.

How many times had he seen each one of these films? Too many to count.

Karen led the way into the bedroom, separated by strands of purple and black wooden beads which hung from the arched doorway.

"So here's my boudoir. You can leave your stuff in here."

Kurt stared at the beaded room divider that was probably left over from the sixties. He carried his belongings through the beaded curtain and placed them down on the floor in front of the bathroom, which was situated across from the bed.

Kurt glanced at a beautifully framed oil portrait he'd painted of Karin when she was around seventeen. It hung over a pale beige futon placed against the wall next to the only window in the entire apartment.

"How did this get here?"

"I had it shipped. I couldn't very well leave my only portrait back in Germany, could I?"

She switched off the overhead light and with a vintage pink metal cigarette lighter lit a pink candle in a frosted pink glass holder on the nightstand next to the futon. The dimly lit room was now pink and alluring.

"Much better," Kurt said.

He threw his arms around her, drew her into a kiss with stored up lust and lifted her black-lace top. Karin gently removed his arms, pulled her top down and stepped away.

"Whoa, there's no need to rush, we have all night and the next night and the next."

"I'm sorry. It's just that it has been two whole months. I thought you felt like me and couldn't wait another minute either."

"Let's have a glass of wine first. I bought your favorite. We should celebrate this occasion, yes?"

"Yes," Kurt said, disappointed, and didn't understand why they weren't tearing each other's clothes off and making love already. Did her passion for him dissipate these last two months?

Karin sauntered over to her kitchen alcove. Kurt trailed behind.

She retrieved a bottle of a respectable Riesling from a small refrigerator, stood on her tiptoes to reach two wine glasses from the cabinet
and set them down on the adjacent yellow speckled Formica counter
top. She poured the wine into the glasses and handed one to Kurt.

He took a sip. "I can't believe we're back together and finally
alone," he said, trying to ignore his worries.

"Me, too," she said softly, but did she really mean it?

She clinked his glass with hers, led him into the bedroom and
they sat on the futon, drinking their wine slowly, kissing each other
tenderly between sips. When their glasses were empty, Karin placed
hers on the nightstand and removed Kurt's from his hand, setting it
down next to hers. He let Karin set the pace.

It was almost as if they were new lovers, discovering each other
for the first time. Karin leisurely undressed Kurt between kisses and
he slowly undressed her. He helped Karin unfold the futon into a bed,
took her hand and they both slid down next to each other. He caressed every part of her body. Each stroke reminded him of how much
he missed her. Kurt gazed at her face and said tenderly, "I love you so
much."

"I know," she said.

Ignoring her chilly response, he moved on top and inside of her
gradually, staring at her closed eyes and taking in her facial expression
as it changed from abandoned to blissful as his pace quickened. He
took special care to make sure she climaxed before he did, which was
something she taught him as a teenager. He remembered how challenging that was at first, but the rewards were innumerable.

After, Kurt held her close to him. His suspicions not quite quelled.

"Did you miss me?" Kurt asked.

"Nah," Karin said, grinning as she slid away from him, moving to
the edge of the bed.

"Where are you going?"

"Just to the bathroom. Do I have your permission to pee, *Herr* Lichter?"

"Perhaps, *Fraulein*."

Karin laughed and hurried over to the bathroom. She almost tripped over Kurt's wooden box. She moved it out of her way with her foot.

"I see you decided to bring this. Does this mean a new portrait of me? I was still a virgin when you painted the last one."

He stared at her skeptically. He was the virgin when they first had sex in their freshman year of high school. She clearly was not.

He sat up. He still couldn't quite believe he was actually in New York and living with her. He was inside a wonderful dream, even if her whole apartment was only slightly larger than his bedroom in Berlin. This would be a totally new experience for them. Sure, they took trips together, many, but not longer than three, four days at a time. And they spent most nights together back in Berlin, but not like this—being together on a daily basis. Was she up to it? Was he?

Karin returned and snuggled beside him. "So you start tomorrow. Nervous?"

"Why should I be?"

"Have you ever really known any Jews? There aren't exactly lots in Berlin. It should be very interesting."

"I don't give a fuck about the Jews. I came here to be with you."

He rolled her over on her back while he moved on top of her again, placing several soft kisses on her head and cheeks. "Now this is what I call interesting,"

She tickled his chest. Her kiss silenced his laughter.

Chapter 5

What do you take me for? Seventy-five? Seventy-nine maybe? Sadie Seidenberg had been known to say to anybody who would listen, daring them to get anywhere close to her actual age, which was eighty-nine. She was a fast walker, a sharp talker, and what some people called "a piece of work".

She was walking down deserted Broome Street at dusk with her next door neighbor, Leon Armstrong. And clearly, too briskly for Leon's taste.

"Sadie, can you slow down a little?" Leon said his voice, hoarse, his breath coming up short. Leon was black, ten years her junior, but unlike Sadie, he looked and acted every moment of his age.

Sadie eyed Leon as he gave himself over to a deep, racking cough. Every Wednesday they shopped together at the Key Food Supermarket, the only large market in the neighborhood. But Sadie could see that those days might come to an end. Soon she might have to shop for the two of them.

"We'd better stop at the pharmacy. You've been sick for weeks now."

Leon brushed her off. "I don't think it's been that long. I'll be all right. It's just a little cold."

"A little cold, my foot. You're very congested. It could be something serious, like with your lungs—what's it called now, COPD. You should go to the doctor already."

"Sadie, you worry too much."

She was about to respond when she spotted two men standing in the doorway of an abandoned apartment building, talking to each other, head to head. Both had black hoodies pulled low over their foreheads, her eyes squinting as she tried to make out their faces. Sadie tightened the grip on the strap of her purse. She was well aware that muggers targeted seniors these days and cast a warning nod at Leon just as the two men sprang at them.

One was taller and older, late twenties or early thirties and looked like a mongrel—a mixture of black and white, multi-racial they called it now. He was hefty with a reddish brown scar on his right cheek. His mouth was shaped like a sneer. She noticed he had a knife.

The shorter younger one looked like he was Puerto Rican and around seventeen or eighteen years of age. He had menacing eyes and a tattoo of a snake spiraling down his neck.

"What do we have here? Walking Miss Daisy?" the taller, older one said, shoving his face right up to Leon, who stood motionless.

"Bangin' Miss Daisy, yo," the younger one said and with one swift move tried to grab Sadie's bag off her shoulder. But Sadie held on.

"Let go, old lady. I don't want to hurt you."

Sadie tried to wrestle her bag away from him, glaring at his snake tattoo that was gold and black, its forked tongue protruding threateningly. The nasty, juvenile mugger gritted his teeth which revealed gold crowns on his two front ones. They jerked the purse back and forth, but she wouldn't let go even when he hurled her to the ground.

She survived worse things than this. Out of the corner of her eye she saw the other man wave his knife at Leon.

"Hand over your wallet, old man."

Leon dug in his pocket, coughing. Sadie yelled, "No, Leon, don't. Don't give them anything."

"Shut up, you old bitch," the man with the knife said.

Leon handed over his wallet. "It's only money, Sadie."

Sadie lay at her assailant's feet, hanging onto the strap of her bag. She managed to grab onto one of his legs with her other arm. He attempted to shake her off, but she had a firm hold.

"Fuck, lady! Let go of your damn bag."

"You want it, cut my arm off. Kill me for it. Go ahead."

"Man, this old lady's fucking nuts. Who needs this shit?"

He let go of Sadie's purse, propelling her onto the pavement. Her arm and leg felt like they had been run over by a tank. Still, she tasted victory; the bag remained clenched in her hand.

The men ran off. Leon hovered over her. "Sadie, Sadie, oh my God . . . oh my God . . . are you okay?"

"I can't move my arm or leg. I feel like I could pass out any minute."

"For Christ sakes, Sadie, he could have killed you. You shoulda let go."

"What and let those *goniffs* take my money? Never."

Leon looked up and down the empty sidewalk.

"Not a soul," he said. "Do you have the cell phone your son gave you?"

"Yes, yes it's still in my purse. I never take it out. It's only for emergencies."

"We have one now. I'll call 9-1-1."

Leon removed the cell phone from Sadie's bag and stifled a cough, his shoulders silently convulsing, while he dialed for help.

Chapter 6

The morning sun blazed through the window onto Kurt and Karin, locked in an embrace, sound asleep. Kurt woke up suddenly, disoriented and groggy from jet lag. He gently untangled himself and checked the clock on the nightstand.

Christ, it's nine o'clock. Damn it.

He stomped over to his duffle bag, dumped out several pair of black jeans and heavy-metal tee shirts and pulled out his one preppy outfit: a pair of tan khakis, a beige Ralph Lauren Polo shirt and a Calvin Klein denim jacket he bought in a secondhand clothing store the last day he was in Berlin. He should make a good impression on his first day, he thought. As he pulled up his pants, he accidently bumped into the bed. Karin opened one eye.

"What's happening?"

"Nothing. I'm fucking late. I was supposed to be there already. Didn't you set the alarm?"

"Calm down, being pissed off is not going to get you there any faster."

He sprinted down the six flights of stairs, tore out of the building to the Astor Place IRT-Lexington subway entrance, descended the steps and hastened up to the token booth, gasping for breath.

"I want one thirty-day MetroCard," he stammered, remembering the instructions he received in Berlin, and handed the clerk several Euros.

"This is the New York City Subway system, buddy, not a bank. We only accept American money."

"*Sich entschuldigung*, I just got here yesterday," Kurt said, taking back the banknote and replacing it with two twenty-dollar bills.

After struggling with the turnstile, Kurt reached the platform. People were stacked ten deep. He'd never seen a crowd like this in Berlin. It looked like the entire city was here. Within seconds a train covered with graffiti arrived. The graffiti in Berlin was very similar to the graffiti here, bold and colorful, except in Berlin it often covered the entire train car, including the windows.

He was shoved into the subway car by the hordes behind him. Riders were jammed without an inch of space between them. Kurt wondered how anyone could breathe. He managed to squeeze his hand onto the overhead bar and was careful not to make eye contact with anyone. He'd heard that New Yorkers could be prickly. He cursed to himself. He was now over an hour late.

Kurt pushed his way out at the Canal Street exit as the doors were closing. Is this what New Yorkers have to go through to get to work every morning, he wondered. That explained why they're so irritable. He ran up the steps and almost tripped over a sleeping homeless man wrapped in blankets. Why don't they have shelters for these people like they do in Berlin, Kurt wondered.

He continued on, noting the street names on each corner. At Henry Street, he checked the address and saw a sign over a storefront: JEWISH SENIORS OUTREACH CENTER.

The large room's walls were covered with posters and photographs of old people posing with young people engaged in arts and crafts, playing cards, singing around a piano. Oh fuck. He gets to hang out with a bunch of old farts when he'd much rather hang out in bed with Karin.

He saw a young man and a young woman, both around his age at work at their out-of-date desktop computers. The young man wore a dark purple crochet skull cap fastened with bobby pins. They were called yarmulkes—this he had learned at the Project Remembrance's training class. This yarmulke was so small it was hardly noticeable as if the guy was hiding the fact that he was a Jew.

At the reception desk, a stocky, gray-haired woman wearing wire-frame granny glasses worked furiously at an ancient adding machine. She looked up. "Can I help you?"

Kurt introduced himself and asked to see David Silver. The woman pointed to a man who seemed to be in his mid-thirties, swarthy complexion with a full beard, dressed in a white, button down shirt and pressed light blue denim jeans—a look that was hip in the nineties but pitiable now. He wore a black satin yarmulke trimmed with red filigree embroidery that looked like it was covering a comb-over from the way his hair was plastered to his longish sideburns.

David was talking excitedly on the telephone; his booming voice filled the room. Kurt couldn't quite follow what David was saying, but it either sounded as if he was enthusiastic or pissed off.

Kurt went over to David's desk and loomed before him, nervously. David put his hand over the receiver. "Kurt Lichter?"

Kurt nodded and David told the caller he would call back and hung up.

"You're very late—one hour and forty-seven minutes to be exact," David said, checking his watch. "Did you get lost on the subways?"

Kurt seized this excuse. "It was very confusing."

"I was about to call the National Guard. Your predecessor,

Wolfgang, as well as all of my other German volunteers, have been very punctual on their first day and from then on. Isn't there an old German adage—promptness is next to Godliness?"

David waited for a response from Kurt but didn't get one. "Anyway, at least you're finally here, but I have to say that Wolfgang is a very tough act to follow. He was extremely valuable to us. Our seniors all loved him like he was their own grandson."

Fuck off! Kurt thought. Wolfgang probably came down with a severe case of pomposity from being around David for almost a year. Being around him for fifteen minutes was long enough.

Kurt stared at David's yarmulke and thought the fancy red embroidery around the rim suited David's personality—superfluous and excessive.

"I'm your first Jew, am I right?" David said, with that same snug smile.

"Oh no. I have seen others, but I've never seen yarmulkes in different styles before and wondered if the various styles of skull caps had any religious significance."

"A yarmulke indicates reverence and humility, a constant reminder that God is above us, in mind and in heart and many Orthodox Jewish men here express their own individuality through them. The younger men even have different ones to match their outfits."

David peered at Kurt as if to say, any other stupid questions? Kurt had none, so David pointed to a table on the other side of the room with coffee, bagels and cream cheese. "Help yourself. We'll start your orientation in a few minutes."

There were a few bagel shops in Berlin, and Kurt had breakfast in one that specialized in "New York bagels" with Karin several months ago when she was determined to sample everything New York style. They'd been bland and hard to chew.

Kurt went over to the refreshment table and picked one up,

dipped it into the cream cheese and bit off a hunk. This bagel tasted so much better. It was darker in color and crustier; the ones in Berlin had tasted like boiled rubber.

He trailed David into a small conference room. Layers of various colors of paint had peeled off the walls and ceiling. David sat in a swivel chair behind an old mahogany desk covered with nicks and scratches. He gestured to Kurt to sit on a metal folding chair across from him.

"I'm sure you have met people with chips on their shoulders, people who are bubbling underneath the surface with anger," he said.

"Yes, I have," Kurt said. "My whole family is like that."

David paused, taking in Kurt's response. "The most important thing to learn about working with Holocaust survivors is that they carry with them the guilt of surviving, when many of their loved ones didn't."

David stopped to give Kurt a look he was becoming used to, a look that said—are you following this or are you as dumb as you look? Kurt nodded and tried to convey intelligence with his eyes. But David wasn't looking at him, he was writing something down on a notepad.

"They also can be extremely paranoid of something happening again that will threaten their security," David continued without looking up from his notepad. "You must be very sensitive to that and not do or say anything that might provoke fear," he said and looked up at Kurt. "And never bring up the Holocaust unless they do, you don't have to be too serious or morbid. Just be yourself, and it never hurts to have a sense of humor."

David put his pen down and smiled, as if smiling and a sense of humor were synonymous. Kurt smiled back but it came out a smirk. He dreaded meeting any survivor of the Holocaust. Tact was never a virtue of his, as Karin had pointed out on many occasions. Given the opportunity, he was sure to say or do the wrong thing.

David handed him several booklets and suggested he read them to give him an understanding of the Jewish religion and also some background on Holocaust survivors and their personality traits.

Kurt concluded that there was an air of superiority and self-righteousness about David Silver. Another crusader. David was definitely convinced he was one of the *Chosen People*.

So was this the trade-off? He'd be with Karin but was going to be surrounded by old fogeys and self-satisfied humanitarians for the next twelve months.

Kurt sat at the dining table, unenthusiastically leafing through *Judaism Today*. He always had trouble concentrating on his reading assignments in school. His mind wandered to fresh ideas for a new painting and Karin often had to summarize the salient points for him, just so he could pass his exams.

He glanced at her, sprawled on the loveseat, reading a book on American filmmakers. Kurt wished he was given a book on film, art or any other subject other than Jews. Bored, he stared out into space.

She sat up abruptly. "This is so American. One day Quentin Tarantino is a clerk in a video store and before you know it, he's a famous filmmaker." She waited for Kurt to respond. When he didn't, she raised her voice. "Kurt, are you listening?"

"What? What is it?"

"I was telling you about Tarantino," she said.

He could tell she was annoyed. "I'm sorry. I can't believe I have to read these stupid things."

Karin put the book down, sashayed over to Kurt and plopped onto his lap. "Do you have to read all of them tonight?"

She tickled his chest. Kurt laughed. She kissed his neck and unbuckled his belt. "I guess your Jews will have to wait."

Kurt tossed the booklet on the floor.

Chapter 7

Kurt walked toward the Jewish Seniors Office, wondering why David had sounded so urgent over the phone and why he wanted him in earlier than his official starting time. Since everyone at the center dressed pretty casually, he wore his usual attire: black leather jacket, black jeans, black high boots, a black tee shirt and his right ear was once again adorned with a Gothic cross.

He walked down East Broadway as shopkeepers hoisted up their awnings, opening up for the day. He noted that Gottlieb and Sons Butchers, Rosensweig's Bakery and Shapiro's Grocery had signs announcing they were kosher, in English and strange letters he assumed were Hebrew. The men were all bearded and had curls instead of sideburns, seemingly dangling from their yarmulkes as if they were sewn on. Kurt exchanged awkward beady-eyed glances with Baker Rosensweig and felt like he was walking through a small village in Eastern Europe, certainly not Manhattan.

On Rivington Street, he passed an old synagogue with two large wooden doors. The bright sun blazed through the large round windows above the doors. Kurt shielded his eyes against the glare and admired the large Stars of David intricately engraved on each glass panel.

He gazed at the magnificence of the sculptured stone doorframe similar to the architecture of many European houses of worship.

The doors opened and an old man with dark, suspicious eyes, in a worn black suit, sporting a plain black yarmulke over his short gray hair, moved toward him. Maybe he's a rabbi, Kurt thought and felt uneasy at the thought of an encounter with a Jewish clergyman. What would he think of a scruffy young German loitering in front of his synagogue. Kurt nodded politely and hurried off. He wanted to avoid being late again.

"I'm sorry, Kurt, I wouldn't do this ordinarily, I mean send you out so soon," David said, his tone more serious than it had been yesterday. "You're not exactly what I would call ready. But, this is an emergency. One of our seniors, Sadie Seidenberg, broke her arm and fractured her leg fighting off a mugger and now needs our help. She's a tough old bird, an Auschwitz survivor."

"You don't have anyone else?"

"No, I'm afraid you're it. She lives in the housing projects not very far from here."

"Like public housing?" Kurt said.

"Yes, but don't worry. It can be somewhat dangerous there at night, but you should be fine during the day."

Kurt panicked. He'd never been in any of Berlin's *Sozialwohnung* except for passing by them to get to somewhere else, but he'd heard they were extremely hazardous.

David seemed to sense his reluctance and, taking a breath, stood up.

"You're from Project Remembrance," David said, "and you're here to perform whatever services we require. That's the deal. Didn't they explain that to you in Berlin?"

"Yes, but . . ." Kurt remained sitting with David towering over him.

"She just needs some of her shopping done, that's all. She was on her way to the market when she was assaulted. Here's the list." He handed it to Kurt along with some money. "You can go to the Key Food Supermarket on Columbia Street. It's on the way to her place. The address and directions are on the back. She'll reimburse you. And remember what I said yesterday—be cheerful but not too cheerful and don't bring up the Holocaust unless she does."

David sat down as Kurt headed for the door.

So this was what he was reduced to—an errand boy. The Lower East Side was definitely the poor side of town. The streets were lined with overflowing garbage cans. Some of its contents spilled onto the pavement; a rank odor polluted the air. Kurt spotted the supermarket on Columbia Street.

Kurt wasn't accustomed to shopping in *Supermarkts*, his mother had always done all the grocery buying as well as the cooking and cleaning. This was unchartered territory for him. He entered the market and grabbed a shopping cart.

The store was large and packed with shoppers who were rushing about as if they were participating in some kind of contest where the first shopper out the door would win lots of money. It seemed like everyone in New York was constantly in a hurry, as if there were amphetamines in the water.

The scolding mothers with their crying children gave him one of his headaches and he had several near misses with other shoppers because the aisles were so narrow that you had to carefully veer your cart around others to avoid collisions.

Even though there were signs in each aisle indicating the products

that were housed there, things were still hard to find as they were all
jammed tightly together on tall shelf units. You had to wait your turn
to get anything because there were so many customers shopping. This
was going take longer than he expected.

He somehow managed to get everything on the list and wheeled
his cart to the front of the store where there were many checkout
counters with long lines. As he was about to stand on a line six deep,
the manager opened up a new register, ushered him to it and he was
able to check out quickly.

Suddenly, he felt lucky. Maybe meeting the old lady wouldn't be
as unpleasant as he thought.

The projects resembled prisons, reminding Kurt of the institutional,
low-income public housing developments in Berlin. He walked into a
large courtyard with a couple of concrete tables with chairs embedded
in the pavement so no one could steal them, he assumed.

He sidestepped two young Puerto Rican boys chasing each other
around a table and walked up to the faded red brick high-rise in the
back of the quad, carrying the three heavy shopping bags, cursing his
fate with every step.

He joined several people waiting for the elevator and moved behind them, avoiding eye contact. A middle-aged Black woman talked loudly on a cell phone. Three seriously tattooed teenage boys, one
Black, one White and one Puerto Rican, shared one cigarette.

New York City. A real hodgepodge. It intrigued him—all these
people, different colors, nationalities and religions, living together in
close proximity. Berlin was the polar opposite. You would see some
brown and black people on the streets and in bars, restaurants and
shops, but rarely mixing together with Germans. At least not yet.

Kurt focused on the metal strip of numbers above the door, which signaled what floor the elevator was on. Only half of them lit up, making the task impossible.

When the doors finally opened, Kurt boarded last and waited until everyone else pressed their floor before he pressed six. He stood in one corner, eyes fixed on the small window in the center of the door.

The elevator rumbled and shook as it headed up and jumped before it stopped on his floor. Kurt was relieved that he got off safely and darted off into a narrow, fluorescent-lit hallway. He knocked at apartment 6A and remembered the meaning of the tarnished, gold mezuzah on the side of the doorframe: a sign of a Jewish household.

He knocked on the door and waited for a few minutes. He set the bags down and knocked harder and heard a faint voice. "I'm coming . . . I'm coming."

The voice got closer and louder. "Hold your horses."

The door finally opened, and there she was, Sadie Seidenberg, a small, wiry old woman with short, wavy gray hair. Her face had wrinkles around her alert hazel eyes and cheeks and her jowls sagged a bit. Yet there was a soft, youthful quality about her, for a woman her age. She wore a faded pastel flowered muumuu under a black cardigan sweater with sleeves pushed up to her elbows. Her right arm was in a cast and a cloth sling, her right leg was in a half-cast, and she held onto a large metal quad cane for support with her good hand. She must have taken quite a beating.

Her critical eyes moved up from his face and down to his toes. Her lips were pursed, as if she just swallowed a lemon. He was sure he failed her inspection.

Kurt glanced at the numbers tattooed on Sadie's left forearm— he'd never seen them in person and watched her quickly pull her sweater sleeve down over the faded black numbers that blurred with the numerous purple veins running down her arm. All he could make out was a two and five.

Oh God, I've done something already to offend her, he thought.

"I'm Kurt Lichter from Project Remembrance," he blurted out.

He noticed her looking at his long hair and his Gothic cross earring.

"You look more like you're from the Hell's Angels," she said. "So come in already, or would you rather stand in the doorway all day?"

Kurt followed her and held up the shopping bags. "Where should I put these?"

"Maybe you should try the kitchen," Sadie said. Kurt noted her sarcasm.

She ushered him through the living room with worn, wall-to-wall sky blue carpeting that had buckled in a few areas, a couch and two matching arm chairs with floral print upholstery covered with plastic, cherry wood tables, family photos everywhere and he thought she must have furnished the room at least fifty years ago. It even smelled old.

On top of a china cabinet was a graduation picture of a beautiful teenage girl with long, wavy reddish-brown hair and hazel eyes like Sadie's. Her engaging smile compelled him to smile back.

He trailed the old woman into her spotless kitchen and noted that her appliances were as outdated as his mother's in Berlin. A yellow speckled Formica table for four with yellow vinyl upholstered chairs sat against the wall across from the refrigerator and stove.

"Put the bags on the table. I'll tell you where everything goes," she said.

Kurt did what he was told and attempted to help her as she slowly maneuvered into a chair.

"Thanks, I can manage by myself," she said, backing away from his outstretched hand.

"But you were hurt."

"You should see the other guy," she said, smirking.

It took him a minute to get her joke. He was usually slow in finding the humor in American wisecracks. By the time he mustered a laugh, the moment had passed. He noted her cold, blank stare. It was clear she didn't like him. As far as he could tell, he'd done nothing wrong yet. He knew helping old people would be a disaster. He clearly didn't have the temperament for it and she wasn't making it any easier.

He took a container of milk and a carton of eggs out of the shopping bag. "What should I do with these?"

"Put them in the refrigerator. What else?"

Again with the sarcasm. He stepped over to the refrigerator with the milk and eggs.

Sadie supervised, gesturing with her cane. "The milk goes on the top shelf. The eggs go on the bottom and be very careful."

"Did you think I was going to juggle them?" Kurt said, thinking that maybe she'd liked his comeback. David had said to have a sense of humor.

Sadie actually thought his joke was funny, but decided to ignore it. When David Silver told her he was sending a young German man from Project Remembrance, she wasn't concerned. She thought highly of the program in theory—young Germans helping survivors of the Holocaust in an act of redemption. She never thought her reaction to this young man would be so negative. She always considered herself open-minded—a true liberal. She liked living in the projects surrounded by people of different races and ethnicities. She didn't expect that a young German's presence would catapult her back to her past.

She regarded Kurt's perfect Aryan face, his black boots just like the ones the Nazi soldiers wore. A face flashed in her mind. A face hidden, buried deep for so long, now had burst forth into her kitchen—her home. She clutched her cane to maintain her balance. It was the face of a young German guard over seventy years ago, eerie blue eyes with a gray tinge that would pierce right through you whenever they happened to glance in your direction, which you hoped they never would. This same guard with the chiseled face would not hesitate to shoot you if you happened to look at him the wrong way. Sadie couldn't figure out what the right way was, so she forced herself to maintain a neutral expression whenever he was nearby.

She struggled to compose herself. That was then and this is now. Those years in the camp emboldened her in a way she never thought possible. She learned one thing that was imperative: You had to be strong to survive. After the war, she swore to herself that she would never again be a victim dependent on another human being's mercy. Never. She became a woman that didn't take crap from anyone. Not from family. Not from friends. Not even from muggers. And now—certainly not from this little *pisher*.

She peered into the two remaining shopping bags and pointed to one of them. Digging into the bag, she took out a box of cold medicine and handed it to Kurt. "Later, you'll take this over to Mr. Armstrong in 6B, just next door. He's got a terrible case of the flu, and then take the bag over to Mrs. Feingold in 6C."

She sensed from Kurt's frown that he was not happy. "She's 92 and in a wheelchair," Sadie said. "I always help her out with a little shopping when her daughter can't do it."

"6B and 6C, okay, anything else?" he said brusquely.

"That's it for now. You must be new at helping people."

She rummaged through the other bag on the table, checking the rest of her groceries to make sure everything she wanted was there. She removed a can of peas, a can of tuna and a box of rice, placed them on the table and gazed at each item.

"I said Del Monte peas, Bumble Bee tuna and Uncle Ben's rice. Wasn't that on the list?" she said, accentuating each brand name.

"It was almost impossible to find anything in that market and these brands were less expensive," Kurt said. "They're the same things. I thought you'd be pleased I saved you some money."

She banged her cane on the floor as if it was a judge's gavel. "No, they're not the same, not the same things at all. What, because I'm Jewish I should only want the cheapest things. I can't spend a few cents more?"

Kurt had no idea what she was talking about. His good intentions were misinterpreted for a second time in the last twenty minutes.

"I'll take them back. Jesus Christ." He slammed the items back in the bag.

"*Mamzer!*" Sadie said sharply.

He didn't know what the word meant, but knew it wasn't complimentary. They locked eyes and he looked away first and hated himself for letting an old biddy get the better of him. He grabbed both shopping bags and stormed off.

His nightmare had started. He'd volunteered for a twelve month stint in Hell.

Chapter 8

"That woman made me lose my appetite," Kurt said, watching Karin serve herself from two large platters of Chinese food and devour the spicy shrimp with string beans and the twice cooked pork with gusto.

"Aren't you going to eat anything?" she said, staring at his empty plate as they sat at a table for two in The Grand Sichuan. It was a small, busy eatery on Mott Street in Chinatown, where the pea-green Formica tables dressed with white paper napkins and chopsticks were so close together, the waiters had to slip sideways between them to serve.

"No, I'm not hungry. Really. Can you believe it? I didn't even know what she was talking about. It was like I was an anti-Semite or something. Stupid old woman. And she lived in a *Gefängnis*—it's like I was found guilty, sentenced, and serving time."

"Forget her. You have to try the shrimp with dried string beans— it's incredible. My film history professor said this is the best Chinese restaurant in New York City. You can't get anything like this in Berlin."

"I can't try anything. I'm not hungry. That damn supermarket gave me the worst fucking headache and if once wasn't enough, I had to go back to the fucking market, get her the brand named shit, then go back again to her house to deliver them."

"You're being ridiculous. What do you care what that old lady thinks?"

"I don't. I don't fucking care."

"Good. Now stop being such *langeiler*. You're with me now. You should be happy."

"You want happy? Here's happy." Kurt pulled his mouth into a toothy smile with his fingers. He sensed her irritation. It was that old Jew's fault. She made him so angry. She was the one spoiling their dinner.

Karin called the waiter over, asked for the check and a doggy bag. When they left the restaurant, she immediately hailed a cab and they headed home in silence, Kurt still mulling over his ordeal, entrenched in his battle with the old woman.

Chapter 9

Sadie sat up in her bed, sipping peach schnapps from a small juice glass to settle her nerves while watching the ten o'clock news. She was determined to keep her attention on the TV even though it was the same gruesome local news as always: Robberies, stabbings, shootings, beatings. Sometimes they caught the suspects, but mostly not.

"*Oy gevalt! Oy vey iz mir!*" Sadie lamented to herself as she did every night, but this night was different. During the commercials, she replayed her interaction with Kurt over and over, as if she'd been asked to testify against him in court and had to remember every single detail. That insolent little *pisher!*

After another few sips of schnapps, she thought maybe she could have acted more maturely, like the adult in the room that she was, and not like the little *pisher's* adversary. She couldn't help herself, her reaction to him was strong and sudden. She hadn't been this agitated in a very long time, eons ago—and it frightened her.

She thought about her husband, Max, and how he would be able to calm her down when she would get overly agitated about whatever small thing upset her that day. He was understated; she was the opposite. While she barged, he retreated. He would always take her in his gentle arms and say in a soft, whispery voice, "*Sadela, my Sadela, is it worth it . . . to get so mad . . . so angry over this nothing, after everything you lived through?*"

She drained her glass, hoping it would make her sleepy. She desperately wanted to shake those ancient feelings and maintain her sanity, her tenacity, which had always served her well. The schnapps finally produced its desired effect. Her eyelids were much too heavy to keep open.

Sadie races through a deserted Berlin street holding the hand of a frail young girl, who trails behind, both wearing tattered black and white striped dresses. They pass a boarded up storefront displaying a charred sign, Teitelbaum's Scheiderei. She can hear footsteps pounding nearby and dogs barking as they scramble closer.

Sadie whispers to the girl, "Please, please mayn shvester, you have to go faster."

The little girl tries her best, panting loudly with each step. She trips over a crack in the pavement and plummets to the ground. Sadie quickly hoists her up, grabs her hand and yanks her along.

Sadie can sense that they're gaining on them. She whips her head around. A Nazi guard draws closer, his long legs sprinting. She's taken countless turns through the streets, yet he has stayed with them. His sniffing dogs must have caught their scent.

Sadie pulls the little girl into an alley. They squat down behind some trash cans and Sadie wraps her arms around her as she starts to cry. She gently covers the girl's mouth with her hand, stifling her sobs.

The guard is so close she can hear him breathing. He stops in front of the cans, his dogs' snouts press against the lids. The guard charges around the bins and points his rifle at them.

Sadie looks up at the guard. His hypnotic blue eyes with a tinge of gray pierce right through her. It's Kurt. He cocks his rifle at the little girl's head and begins to squeeze the trigger.

"So you think you can run and hide from me, Frauleins?"

Sadie sat up and placed a hand on her own pounding heart as if her hand alone could keep it from exploding. Her nightgown was drenched in sweat as if she'd been running for miles. A mixture of sorrow, terror and rage that she thought had vanished took hold of her.

Oh my God, the nightmares, they're starting again!

Chapter 10

Kurt hovered over David's desk like a rain cloud. He could hardly contain his anger.

"An old bird? That woman is a vulture. She took an immediate disliking to me. I couldn't do anything right and she had me delivering things to the whole building. Isn't there anything else I can do?"

"I don't know what you expected, Kurt, but this is what you signed up for," David said sharply. "You can work here in the office for now, I can use some help with the filing, but later you'll have to go back to Mrs. Seidenberg to take her and her neighbor, Mrs. Feingold, to Friday night services. I told her you would be bringing her and she didn't complain."

"You mean at a church, I mean, a synagogue?" Kurt said. Should a German Catholic be going to a Jewish service? He regretted even thinking about joining Project Remembrance. He had to remind himself that the only reason he put himself in this torturous situation was to be with the love of his life, and he accomplished that.

David leaned in. "I know from working with others from your organization that there are very few Jewish communities in Germany now. Even though your group provided you with some essential knowledge, there are a lot of Jewish traditions that are not generally known among young Germans. It's okay. By the end of your time here you'll become very well informed."

It was obvious that David was not pleased with him either. His first week in New York and he'd already fucked up his first encounter with a Holocaust survivor and his relationship with his Jewish boss. At least he had Karin.

David glared and raised his eyebrows at Kurt's black leather jacket over a black tee shirt, tight black jeans and his dangling Gothic cross. "And, Kurt, if you can, please change what you're wearing now. It's true that the young people don't dress up for Synagogue anymore, but you look a little too punkish for Friday night services and for God's sake, remove your earring. I'm not sure my congregation would know what to make of your Gothic cross."

Kurt entered the empty apartment. Karin was at her Film History class and wouldn't be back until early evening. Too bad, she was much better at putting together more conservative outfits as she dressed up often for her family's special occasions.

He trudged into their so-called bedroom, feeling miserable. Karin's musky, warm spicy scented perfume saturated the air. He instantly felt better. He took a deep breath through his nose and was overpowered by the sensuous aroma. He closed his eyes and imagined her lying on the bed, naked, waiting for him.

It had been a few nights since they last made love, before their dinner in Chinatown, before his altercation with Sadie. He was consumed with resentment. He wasn't up to making love, both literally and figuratively. His moods sometimes interfered with his libido. Karin usually cajoled him out of them, but this time she didn't try.

He foraged through his clothes in the one drawer that Karin had provided for him. He grabbed his one pair of khakis, a navy blue wool turtleneck as it got much colder at night now, and changed into them. He'd have to wear his leather motorcycle jacket even though it wasn't appropriate—it was the only warm jacket he had. And what about his fucking shoes? He only had his boots and a worn, dirty pair of sneakers. Maybe he could wear his boots under his khakis? He sat on the futon and pulled up one boot under his pant leg. Thankfully, they were wide leg pants. Amazing. He then quickly put on the other boot. It worked perfectly. *Wunderbar!*

He couldn't fucking believe it—he was dressing for church—a Jewish church at that. The sacrifices one makes for love.

He went into the bathroom and gazed at Karin's skimpy black lace negligee hanging from a hook on the door. He pictured her posing seductively in it, looking like she just stepped out of a Victoria's Secret catalogue.

Kurt removed his earring and tried his best to slick back his hair with Karin's hair styling gel so he would look more presentable and checked himself out in the floor length mirror that hung outside of the bathroom door. Even though his outfit was a bit mismatched, it was good enough.

He went into the kitchen, found one of her notebooks on the table and quickly ripped out a sheet of paper. He jotted down where he would be for the evening as she'd be expecting him to be there when she got back. Why worry her unnecessarily?

Dusk had fallen over the Lower East Side when Kurt returned to Sadie Seidenberg's apartment. His stomach knotted as he entered the building. The elevator was already there as if it was waiting for him.

He dreaded seeing the old woman again. The last time he saw her was when he brought back the name brands that she'd originally requested from her grocery list. She'd greeted him like he was some unsavory, long lost relative, who unexpectedly showed up at her door out of the blue. She snatched the bag from his hand without so much as a smile or a "hello" or a "thank you" and then shut the door in his face. He hoped for a better reception this time.

He watched the passing floors through the small window as it ascended to the sixth floor. His anxiety increased with each level. He had no idea how he would be received.

When he knocked, Sadie immediately opened the door as if she'd been waiting behind it. Bundled up in a puffy black down coat with a long striped black and white wool knit scarf wrapped around her neck and a matching black and white knit hat pulled down below her ears, she looked like she was about to head off on an expedition through the Arctic Circle. All she needed was a dog sled with three huskies leading the way. He had to bite his lip to stifle his laugh.

"You're fifteen minutes late. We still have to get Mrs. Feingold. Rabbi Feldman is not going to wait for us, you know," Sadie said.

She stared at his attire and his hair. It seemed like she almost approved of his appearance. Her face was a little less sour than before. She grabbed her cane which was hanging from a coatrack near the door and led Kurt two doors down and knocked. Mrs. Feingold told them to come in. She sat in her wheelchair with her camel hair coat on, ready to go.

"Oh, Sadie, you just missed my Ruthie. She was dying to see you," Mrs. Feingold said at full volume. Kurt noticed a hearing aid lodged in her right ear. He didn't remember her wearing one when he dropped off her groceries a couple of days ago.

"I'm so sorry, but I was waiting for Leonardo Di Caprio here,"

Sadie said in a louder voice than usual, most likely so Mrs. Feingold could hear her.

At least Leonardo Di Caprio was a step up from the Hells Angels. All he had to do was drop the two old bags at the synagogue and return home to his sexy Karin.

Kurt pushed Mrs. Feingold's wheelchair down the sidewalk. After several blocks, she had dozed off and was snoring softly. Sadie held onto his arm with one hand and led the way with her cane in the other, begrudgingly silent.

Two aging punk rockers with pastel hair walked toward them and stared at the unlikely threesome. Their faces seemed contorted with suppressed laughter. As they passed, Kurt felt embarrassed to his core. He quickened his pace, practically sprinting. Sadie yanked his arm. "Slow down a little, what is this, the Special Olympics? Turn at the next corner and go down one more block."

He was thankful that no one else noticed them and was relieved when he spotted the old synagogue, the same one he had admired a few days earlier. He stopped to study the filigree stone work above the doors.

"You don't see workmanship like this anymore," Sadie said.

"No, you don't. Even in Europe the newer churches are very modern."

Kurt looked at all the people going in. He felt like an intruder and wondered if these Jews could tell he was a German Catholic. If they knew, would they care?

A man in his late sixties, wearing a faded blue uniform held the door open for them. "*Gut Shabbos,*" he said.

"Who's that?" said Kurt.

"It's Ben Levine. He used to be a security guard before he retired. Now he's our volunteer guard."

Kurt was surprised to hear that a small synagogue like this would need protection. He escorted Sadie and Mrs. Feingold down the aisle, gaping at an exquisite mural depicting scenes from the Old Testament. It wrapped around the entire wall. Although some sections were faded and crumbling, it was still striking. The colors were dark and rich. The brush strokes were short, blending one tone into another, creating an illusion of depth.

Kurt studied each panel meticulously. The first one depicted Baby Moses in a basket of bulrushes in the Nile River. A woman with a sweet, compassionate smile on her face, in a white draped dress with multi-colored jewelry, reached into a brown basket almost hidden by tall muted green grass. She was flanked by two brown slaves in white loincloths standing in aquamarine rippling water under a pale blue sky.

The second panel showed Moses and the burning bush. The colors were dark and menacing. A terrified Moses, wearing a burgundy robe and head scarf, knelt before a brown bush engulfed in bright orange and yellow flames, with arms stretched toward the blaze. Charcoal gray smoke billowed over a mountainside, covered with gray rocks, outlined in black paint.

His eyes then fixed on Moses leading the Hebrews through the desert. An older, beleaguered Moses, wearing a brown robe and a white headdress, with a flowing, gray beard, held a long staff as he trekked through yellowish, beige sands. A band of Hebrews (men, women and children) followed him, wearing multi-colored robes under a blue-gray sky.

Kurt then examined Moses parting the waters. Moses, wearing a red garnet robe and headdress, pointing to the parted blue-green ocean with bubbles of white foam bursting from the brim of where the waters were split in two, providing a path for him and his followers to trek through. His flock turned to him with outstretched arms as they began to follow behind him on their way toward the promised land.

The last one was Moses receiving the Ten Commandments on Mount Sinai. An anguished Moses with wind-blown white hair and beard, holding a long brown staff in one hand and two carved stone tablets under his other arm. He stood on a gray rock ledge, wearing a long faded white robe draped with a long red cape, under a lightning struck, red-orange sky, which gave the ledge and sky a golden glow.

Each scenario was rendered in such vivid detail that Kurt felt surrounded by Moses and his flock.

"Magnificent, isn't it," Sadie said.

"Oh yes, brilliant. It almost looks three dimensional, and what rich colors. It reminds me of Italian Renaissance painting."

"Sounds like you studied art," Sadie said.

"Yes, a little." He didn't feel like discussing his years at art school with the old lady. It was too painful to disclose to a stranger. His eyes darted nervously around the room and he saw David nod at him. He nodded back politely.

"Take us over there," Sadie said, pointing to some seats on the end of a row toward the middle. She tapped Mrs. Feingold's shoulder and awakened her. "You can park Mrs. Feingold in the aisle."

Mrs. Feingold flashed a warm smile at Kurt and thanked him. He led them over and helped Sadie into her seat. "Come back for us in an hour," she said. "The service should be over by then."

Kurt nodded and hurried up the aisle as David intercepted him. "You're leaving?"

"Yes. Mrs. Seidenberg told me . . ."

"My volunteers from your group usually stay for the services—to learn firsthand about the Jewish religion. *Shabbat* is the most important ritual observance in Judaism."

"Look, man, I don't even go to Christian services."

David ignored his protest and handed him a prayer book and a yarmulke. "Please sit with Mrs. Seidenberg. Who knows? You might even enjoy it."

Kurt felt strange holding the skull cap and thought it might be offensive for a German to be wearing it.

"It's just a religious service, Kurt. It's not like going to the dentist," David said.

I'd rather go to the dentist, he thought.

David gestured to him to put on the yarmulke and hurried off to sit in the front row.

Kurt stepped down the aisle and squeezed in next to Sadie.

"You're going to stay for the services?" she said.

"Yes, David insisted."

Kurt placed the yarmulke on top of the prayer book and held them both firmly in his lap. Sadie tapped him on his shoulder and gestured to the skull cap. "What are you waiting for—a written invitation? Put it on."

"It goes right on top of your *kop*," Mrs. Feingold said, pointing to his head.

"Maybe I shouldn't be wearing it," he said, afraid he would antagonize the Jews after all they suffered at the hands of the Germans.

"What? You think you'll become a Jew by wearing a yarmulke? You're in a synagogue, for God's sake. It's a sign of respect," Sadie said.

Once again she misinterpreted his intentions. He contained his anger and stuck it on top of his head. It tilted to one side. Sadie adjusted it so it sat in the center. "It's not a beret."

He opened the book to the first page.

"Hebrew is written from right to left—back to front," Sadie said, turning to the last page of his book. "You begin reading here."

Kurt felt like he was dropped on another planet and wished someone would send him back to earth.

A man stepped up to the podium wearing a black suit with a white silk fringed shawl wrapped around his shoulders. Kurt recognized him as the old man he saw a few days earlier. I hope he doesn't notice me, he thought.

The rabbi began the service by lighting the Sabbath candles. "*Baraukh atah Adonai Eloheinu, melakh ha'olam,*" he said.

The congregation recited the prayer with the rabbi, whose voice was warm, his smile inviting. Kurt sat for the rest of service as if he was embedded in a block of ice. He hadn't been inside a house of worship since he was an adolescent and raised such a fuss his parents stopped demanding that he go. The chapel had a large statue of a bloodied Jesus on the cross, and it always frightened him. As a child he had recurring nightmares in which a menacing Jesus came to life and stalked him through the pews.

Kurt ran up the front steps of Karin's building, rushed up the stairs and opened the door. He expected to see her waiting for him, eager to hear about his day, but instead he found a darkened apartment. He switched on the light, found a note on the kitchen table, scribbled on the back of his note to her. It had the name and address of a bar, University Pub, 11 Waverly Place in the West Village. It said to meet her there and included walking instructions.

Where was she? After his excruciating experience at the synagogue, all he wanted was to get plastered and laid. He quickly changed into his usual outfit and left the apartment, slamming the door behind him.

As soon as he hit the street it began to shower, a light sprinkling at first, which quickly turned into a heavier downpour, timed perfectly just to really piss him off. New York was like that: one minute it was sunny and in the next, the sky would darken and open, releasing heavy rains, cleansing the grimy city streets instantaneously.

He pulled his jacket as far as he could over his head and kept his face down to protect himself. He sprinted north up to First Avenue and then East on Tenth and stuck close to buildings, under awnings, shielding himself from the rain. He passed bodegas, dive bars, ethnic restaurants and the usual East Village crowd: young hipsters, old hippies, looking like they were time travelers from the sixties, aging punk rockers with pastel colored hair with gray roots, multiple piercings and exotic tattoos; all trying to stay dry by placing anything handy over their heads. He savored the strange assortment of weirdos. In Berlin you would rarely encounter such an array of humanity walking shoulder to shoulder in one neighborhood, but these streets were heterogeneous. He felt surprisingly comfortable, blending in perfectly with all the other misfits.

When he reached St. Mark's Place, he ducked under the marquee of the Orpheum Theater. He moved his head from side to side frantically in a feeble attempt to shake the rain out of his hair and dug into his pocket. He grabbed the paper with the directions and noted the path he was to follow: St. Mark's Place toward Third Avenue, slight left onto Broadway, right onto Waverly Place onto Washington Square, continue onto Waverly.

Fuck! Why the hell did he have to walk all the way to West Village with a left here and a right there, when there were plenty of cool bars near where they lived. At least the rain had softened a bit, returning to a gentle spray.

He began his journey west, noting that this would be his first time in Greenwich Village, even though he'd been in New York for almost a month. He'd seen it many times in American movies, marveling at how European it looked with its late 1800's, early 1900's brownstones and narrow tree-lined streets. He'd been meaning to get there, but since he had arrived in New York City, he was trapped between the East Village and the Lower East Side.

After he passed Astor Place, he trekked onto Broadway and then onto Waverly, where the crowd changed to a mixture of university students and tourists, mostly Asians with cameras hanging from their necks, and trendy young couples. The apartment buildings, shops and restaurants were more upscale as compared to their counterparts in the East Village.

Kurt spotted the bar and couldn't believe that he had to hike all the way in the rain to end up here—a fucking typical college hangout. He weaved his way through a group of kids wearing NYU sweatshirts, smoking cigarettes under a sign that said smoking permitted here, and entered the noisy, crowded place. The guy at the door checking IDs stared at him incredulously, as if he'd stumbled into the wrong bar.

Inside, the young university students all seemed to resemble each other and the pub had a chic, trendy feel, with a long mahogany bar, polished to a brilliant shine with matching paneled walls—the polar opposite to his seedy hangouts in Berlin. Here, he didn't blend in.

Kurt noticed Karin at a booth in the rear with two men. He hung back. The man beside her looked like he was in his mid-twenties and he wore his long sandy brown hair in a ponytail. The man across from her sported a well-groomed black goatee interspersed with a few stray gray hairs. A large half-full pitcher of beer sat in the middle. Karin's mug was almost empty.

Kurt wasn't sure what was going on, but he didn't like it. Karin was giggling too loudly, touching the arm of the ponytailed man and smiling playfully at the one with the goatee. He had seen this outrageous, flirtatious behavior before, usually when she drank too much. He stepped over.

"Karin," he said.

She seemed unperturbed by the interruption. "Kurt came all the way from Germany just to be with me," she told the men without missing a beat. She grabbed his hand. "Isn't that right, Kurt?" she asked, and then wiped her hand with a napkin. "Were you caught in that downpour?"

Kurt didn't answer and shifted back a step.

She gestured to the man with the goatee. "This is my film history professor, Brent Hoffman. He wrote a famous book about the American film renaissance in the sixties and seventies."

She cocked her head to the ponytailed guy. "And this is Adam Walker, a fellow graduate film student. He's doing his thesis on the rise and fall of independent American cinema."

The men nodded courteously. Kurt didn't respond. Karin swigged the last of her beer. "Kurt, why are you just standing there like a statue? Sit next to Brent," she said.

Brent tentatively moved over, but Kurt didn't budge. He had no desire to join this threesome.

"Brent, Adam—this is Kurt Lichter. Kurt used to be a very talented artist. Now, the only brush he uses is the one for his hair," she said, pointing to his head, laughing. She appeared to relish the awkwardness of the moment.

Kurt snatched her outstretched arm. "What the fuck is wrong with you?" he said, tightening his grip.

Brent moved to the edge of the booth and reached for Kurt's hand. "Hey, chill out."

Kurt seized Brent's arm and accidentally pushed it into the

pitcher, tipping it over and spilling beer all over the table and the floor. Seconds later a couple of waiters appeared with mops.

Another waiter hurried over to Kurt, took his arm and pulled him away from the table. "Hey, man. We don't allow this in here."

"I was just leaving anyway," Kurt said and turned to Karin. "*Fich dich, Schlampe!*"

Kurt rolled over from his stupor, opened one eye and spotted two empty Thunderbird bottles lying on the floor, next to the bed. He glanced over at Karin's side of the bed. Empty. With much effort, he turned his head toward the clock and checked the time. *Verdammt!* It was four in the morning. Where the fuck was she? He grabbed the bearer of bad news, threw it onto the floor and rolled over and fell back dead asleep.

He was awakened by the alarm screeching from its new position on the floor. It was 7 a.m. Karin hadn't returned. He plodded over to the clock and shut it off, grabbed the clothes he wore yesterday off of the floor and put them on.

Chapter 11

Sadie opened the door and, instead of saying hello or good morning, directed Kurt next door to 6B, Leon Armstrong's apartment. She grabbed her cane off of the coatrack.

"Poor Leon, he can't seem to get over his cold. We have to look in on him," she said, handing Kurt a key ring with a blue plastic "S" dangling from it. "I have a key exchange policy with Leon and Mrs. Feingold in case of an emergency. They're color coded. Here, open Leon's door with the keys that have the red caps."

He didn't have the energy to argue or complain. He followed Sadie down the hallway, plagued by the thought of Karin sleeping with one of those men from last night, and was still furious at her for humiliating him in front of them.

Kurt lagged behind while Sadie hurried into Leon's bedroom. Kurt glanced at a weathered brown corduroy couch, a beige imitation leather recliner and a laminated mahogany coffee table piled high with a week's supply of newspapers and magazines piled on top. A typical man's living room—just the basics, nothing fancy, and messy, reminding him of his bedroom back home.

He caught up with Sadie. The gloomy bedroom smelled like

cough medicine and dirty socks. Leon smiled when he saw Sadie, but was interrupted by a brief coughing attack. Sadie started to introduce the two men, but Leon reminded her with a dismissive wave of his hand that he'd already met Kurt when he delivered the cough medicine.

She placed her hand on Kurt's arm. "Go into the kitchen—it's through the living room and to the left, the same as my place. Get a spoon from the top right hand drawer next to the fridge and hurry back."

When he returned, he noticed that the window had been opened, allowing a cool breeze to air out the room. Sadie must have noticed the smell, too, he thought.

She told Kurt to fill the spoon with cough medicine and then hand it to Leon. Leon attempted to swallow the medicine, but his coughing made it impossible. Kurt flinched and turned away, avoiding the spray from Leon's mouth.

Sadie jabbed Kurt's leg with her cane. "For crying out loud, just give him some water."

Leon tried to speak, but was unable to stop coughing.

"He's spitting right into my face," Kurt said and picked up a glass of water on Leon's nightstand and held it up to Leon's mouth. Not taking any chances, Kurt turned his face in the opposite direction. Leon ceased hacking and took a drink.

"Lord have mercy, I have a Yiddisher mama at my age," Leon said, handing Kurt the empty spoon.

Kurt filled the spoon and brought it up to Leon's mouth, but Leon spit it up all over him. Kurt jumped back, spilling water onto the bed. Leon continued to cough uncontrollably.

Sadie poked Kurt with her cane. "Get him another glass of water before he chokes to death. And get a towel for God's sake."

Kurt ran out of the room and into the kitchen. He grabbed a roll of paper towels on the counter, tore off several sheets and wiped the cough syrup off of his shirt but it only made it worse; the stain spread. He couldn't believe being stuck in this position. It wasn't bad enough being a delivery boy, now he was a fucking nurse.

He filled the glass, rushed into the bathroom, grabbed a towel and hurried back into the bedroom. He held the glass of water up to Leon's mouth, and the old man was finally able to drink it. Kurt placed the glass on the nightstand, took the medicine from Sadie, and filled the spoon with another dose. This time, Leon successfully swallowed it and thanked Kurt profusely for all his help.

"We better let Leon get some rest," Sadie said and turned to Leon. "I'll look in on you later. If you need anything, you call me."

Kurt trailed Sadie out of the bedroom and out of the apartment.

"Don't forget to lock the door with the red key," Sadie said, handing him her key ring.

He locked the door and turned to her. "Now, I've got that man's germs all over me. I'm going to get sick, thanks to you, and that damn medicine will never come out of my clothes."

"Like you're wearing an Armani suit," she said. "You're young and healthy—you won't come down with anything, trust me."

Kurt stomped down the hallway ahead of Sadie. "I'm supposed to be helping you," he shouted. "Not everybody else in the world. What are you, the Jewish Mother Theresa?"

"Do me a favor and don't come back," she yelled, matching his volume. "I'll get someone else to help. I don't need this aggravation."

Chapter 12

Kurt headed home, replaying his argument with Sadie. He knew his behavior was excessive. His temples throbbed and his heart pounded thinking about where Karin might be and what she might be doing. He suspected she was growing apart from him in the last couple of weeks. Sure, they had their spats before, but she was always faithful to him, or so he thought.

His hands curled into fists as he climbed up the front steps. His breath came up short as he ascended the six flights of stairs. He managed to steady his hand just long enough to get the key in the lock. He swung the door open and marched in, tripping over his duffle bag.

"*Was zum teufel*," he shouted. He stared at his belongings, stunned. His paint box had been placed beside the bag.

Struggling to catch his breath, he trudged forward and peered at Karin, sprawled out on the couch, engrossed in Scorsese's *Taxi Driver* for what he thought might be the hundredth time. She sat up, and clicked her remote on pause.

"What's going on?" Kurt yelled, but he knew exactly what was happening.

"I packed your things," she said, sliding off the loveseat, moving toward him.

Her words knocked whatever air he had left in his lungs. He felt his legs buckling beneath him, yet was able to remain upright.

He could feel his face burning up. "What? Why?" he said.

"I don't think our living together is right for me just now," she said unceremoniously.

Her monotone voice intensified his pain. "You wanted me to come here—we planned it together."

"I know. I thought it would be like it used to be."

"So what changed?"

"You and your goddamn temper. You've been angry since day one. All you do is bitch about that old Jew and fight with everyone," she said.

She had that look on her face he knew only too well. She'd come to a conclusion and was determined to carry it out. He knew he couldn't change her mind, but couldn't help himself from trying.

"I always had a temper—you knew that. You used to love my temper. My fire, you called it."

"You don't even paint any more," she said, touching his arm. "When was the last time you picked up a brush or a piece of charcoal?"

"I just can't do it right now. You know why. You know all about that," he said, backing away. Just as he suspected, she brought up his painting, or lack of it, like every time she'd been angry at him this past year.

"All I know is that our lives are going in different directions," she said. "And we'll always be friends. You can call me whenever," Karin said, stepping closer.

She used that soft, condescending tone of voice that she used whenever she felt sorry for him.

"You met someone else, one of those men from the other night. The professor?"

Karin lowered her eyes.

"I joined that stupid organization so I could come to New York to be with you. Now what the hell am I supposed to do? I'm stuck here for another eleven months working with these crazy old Jews."

"I'm sorry. Maybe you . . ."

"Maybe what?" he said, leaning in. "Go back to Berlin? Tell my mother she was right about you and me? Never. And even if I wanted to go back, I can't. I have no fucking money," Kurt said, staring at her watery eyes. Her tears made him angrier. He kicked his paint box toward her feet.

"Maybe you can get a job," she said softly.

"On whose visa? Yours? Mine's only good if I stay with that group. I have to finish out my goddamn term. Why the hell are you doing this to me?" he said, shocked at the blankness in her face.

He grabbed his belongings, stomped out, not bothering to close the door. He raced down the six flights and out of the building. At least he'd never have to climb those damn steps again.

He roamed Second Avenue, looking for a working payphone. The ones he found either had colored wires hanging out where the receiver used to be, or had the receiver dangling from the phone with no dial tone. The payphones have all died, he thought. I must be the only person in New York who doesn't have a fucking cell phone.

Finally, he saw a phone booth inside Arnie's Luncheonette. Straight out of a fifties movie complete with a soda fountain and red vinyl covered booths. He walked in, scrounged inside his pocket and pulled out a quarter, set down his duffle bag and dialed. "Hello, David, it's Kurt. Do I still have access to my accommodations?"

Kurt plodded into the 92nd street YMHA (Young Men's Hebrew Association) as if he was going to face his execution. She should have just stuck a knife in his back, it would have hurt less.

At the front desk, the clerk, wearing a Pearl Jam tee shirt, strummed an unplugged electric guitar in accompaniment to a hard rock tune playing softy on a tape recorder.

Kurt cleared his throat. The desk clerk looked up at Kurt, turned off the music and put down his guitar. "Sorry, I have a gig later."

He told the clerk his name and that he worked for David Silver.

"Oh yeah, I just got a call from him. He told me you would be arriving," he said and extended his hand to Kurt. "Antonio Giancarlo Rosenberg at your service."

Kurt raised his eyebrows, shaking his hand briefly.

"Call me Tony. I'm half Italian and half Jewish," he said. "On my father's side, I've got Jewish guilt and on my mother's, Catholic guilt. So you might say that I'm guilty on two counts."

Kurt was too devastated to smile.

"Hey, man, you okay? I usually get a big laugh from that line."

"I've been better."

"Anyway, you have room 501. That was Wolfgang's room, from your organization also. He was totally different from you—a real preppy looking dude," Tony said, handing him a key. "Each floor has a communal bathroom and kitchen. The house rules are posted on the back of the door. Don't worry, your luxurious accommodations should cheer you right up. I should know. I'm not only an employee, I'm also a tenant. The elevators are to your left."

Tony seemed like the kind of person he could connect with. He had just the right balance of wit and sarcasm. It would be nice to have a friend for a change.

He joined several young men waiting for the elevator, speaking a language he wasn't able to identify. He guessed from their swarthy complexions and aquiline noses that they were probably Israelis.

Everywhere he went he was surrounded by Jews; there was no escaping them.

In the elevator, Kurt sensed all eyes were on him, probably wondering who he was and why he was there. The men nodded at Kurt and he nodded back. When he got off, one of them held the door open for him and Kurt bowed his head and said "*Shalom,*" remembering from somewhere that it was a Hebrew word used as both a greeting and a farewell. As the door closed, Kurt heard the men laughing. Maybe it was his German accent.

He hiked down the long, narrow, brightly fluorescent hallway and opened his door. The bland room was in desperate need of color, everything was beige or white. It was the same size as his room back in Germany with a single bed and one pillow, a laminated blond wooden dresser, desk and chair, and a closet with a couple of plastic hangers. At least it was clean.

He walked over to the window and looked out on Lexington Avenue, feeling like he'd been given a prison sentence and this was his cell.

He read the house rules posted on the back of the door. No smoking anywhere. You could have an overnight guest of either sex, but it cost fifteen dollars and they could only stay three nights within a seven-night period. Who the fuck cared? It was last thing he wanted. He was done with women.

He threw his duffle bag and paint box on the floor. He dropped down on the bed, sinking into it. He jumped up as he felt something in his back pocket—Sadie's key ring. Shit! He'd have to face her again.

He opened his paint box, gazed at its neglected contents and hurled it onto the floor. The ancient paint tubes rolled sideways and then lay still. A half-used bottle of paint thinner somersaulted out of the box, landing face down. The old, hardened brushes scattered on the floor like fallen soldiers.

He pitched his duffle bag onto his bed and dumped its contents. A framed photograph of Karin landed on his pillow. She'd actually packed a picture of herself. What the fuck for? Her vanity enraged him. He snatched it up and smashed it against the wall. Shards of glass rained all over the room.

Chapter 13

Sadie jerked up the window shade in her kitchen, watching it whirl to the top. The sun shone brightly, highlighting the bald spot on the back of Jack's head, casting a yellow glow that resembled a halo as he sat at the table. Sadie laughed to herself. She'd never thought of her only child as being angelic before.

Sitting across from him, she sipped her tea and watched as he drank his coffee, meticulously wiping his mouth with his napkin after each swallow. She admired his charcoal pinstripe suit, probably a Gucci or Prada or some other fancy designer. Her son had impeccable taste in clothing even before he became a successful lawyer.

Rebecca was preparing a salad at the counter. With her wavy, shoulder-length brunette hair, Sadie's grandchild reminded her of the girl in the granola bar commercials, walking in the woods with a waterfall backdrop, the perfect image of natural wholesome beauty.

"First day of med school and I already have a month's worth of studying," Rebecca said, slicing tomatoes with remarkable precision.

"It's a good thing we're going to have a doctor in the family now that your grandmother here has decided to be the next Charles Bronson," Jack said, dabbing his chin with his napkin. "Come to think of it, Don King needs a new fighter; maybe I should introduce the two of you," he said to Sadie. "I met him once at a Boys and Girls Club fund raiser."

She shot him a look reserved for his smart-alecky comment. "I should give those hoodlums my money? Never."

"Next time use the pepper spray I got you, slugger."

"I squirted it in my chicken soup. It was very tasty."

"For God's sake, Mom, you could have been killed. How many times do we have this same conversation? You can live anywhere you want. What about that wonderful place in Florida where your cousin Yettie lives? You know I'll pay for it," he said. Noting Sadie's grimace, he changed his strategy. "Or I can find you a nice place near me in Beverly Hills," he said, finishing his coffee.

Sadie stared at her son with a mixture of love and frustration.

"Sure, what about right next door to the Kardashians," she said, placing her hand over his. "I know you're an important lawyer now, but you're my son, not my boss, and this is where I want to live. This is where your father, may he rest in peace, and I lived—where we raised you. My friends are here. My synagogue is here."

Rebecca set the salad bowl in the center of the table. "Okay, you two, can we call a truce and have lunch?"

Jack gently touched his daughter's arm. "None for me, sweetheart. I have to catch my plane."

Rebecca filled her grandmother's bowl.

"It's like a dream come true having you here in New York City," Sadie said, gazing at her granddaughter with adulation. "I can't believe that I'll get to see you more than just a couple of times a year. What a gift," she said, spreading her napkin on her lap.

Rebecca leaned over, wrapped her arms around Sadie's shoulders and gave her a kiss on her cheek, then sat in between her grandmother and her father.

"Daddy, you have to go right now? Your plane isn't for five hours. Are you walking to the airport?" she said, serving herself.

"I have a meeting before I go," he said and dug his fork into the salad bowl, plucked out a tomato slice and some turkey and devoured it. He wiped his mouth with his napkin and pulled out a travel-sized breath spray from his jacket pocket and shot a healthy dose into his mouth.

He reached across the table and touched Rebecca's hand. "Oh, that reminds me," he said. "I left some pepper spray for you on your dresser. I also gave your doorman season tickets to the Knicks, so he'll keep an extra eye out for you."

"Great. I'm probably the only medical student living in a luxury apartment with a bodyguard," she said.

"This is New York City, not a gated community. I'm not taking any chances," he said, rising. He went over to counter and poured himself another cup of coffee.

"I can't believe you live in another city now," he said, staring at his daughter with what appeared to be sincere emotion as he returned to the table.

"And I can walk and talk and feed myself, too," Rebecca said.

Jack sat down, added a drop of cream to his coffee. "I know, I know—but, this is the first time you're living away from home. NYU med school was your idea, not mine."

"I'll be fine, Dad. Really. After all, Grandma's here, she'll protect me," Rebecca said jokingly, gesturing toward Sadie.

"I don't have a black belt for nothing, you know," Sadie said.

"Why do you think I'm so worried?" Jack said and turned his head toward Rebecca. "Seriously, call me every night, just so I don't worry. At least to start with."

He paused for a moment and took a deep breath. "And, sweetheart,

I took the liberty of giving Milt Goodman your phone number. His son, Josh, goes to Columbia. He made law review last year. Milt and I thought the two of you might get along. I met Josh a couple of times and he's a fine boy."

Sadie stared at her son and then at Rebecca and braced herself for the ensuing flare-up.

"Daddy, you're making a match for me already. I've just started med school," Rebecca said, raising her voice.

"Who said anything about a match—it would be just someone to go out with. You don't know anyone here besides your grandmother. I thought you'd be happy," he said, and then looked at Sadie pleadingly for support. "Did I do such a terrible thing?"

Sadie shrugged. "I'm not one to interfere."

"Daddy, you're meddling again. I can't believe it. You know how I feel about that. Can you remember one boy you fixed me up with that I liked? Anyway, I'm going to be too busy to date."

"Well he's going to call you. It won't hurt to have dinner with him at least once and if I remember correctly, your choices haven't always been the best—like that rock musician who looked like a derelict and was always borrowing money from you."

Sadie remained silent. This was none of her business. She knew how protective her son was with his daughter, but given the circumstances, she understood. Jack had been both mother and father to his daughter for the last seven years and it had taken its toll on the both of them.

He checked his watch and immediately stood up. "Anyway, I've got to go now or I'll be late." He walked over to Sadie and gave her a cursory kiss on her forehead.

"Take care, Mom. I'm sorry, but I really have to go. I'll call you soon."

Sadie patted his arm.

"Goodbye, Dad, and have a safe trip," Rebecca said and cast him a hostile look as he left the kitchen.

"This salad is delicious—I'm on my second bowl," Sadie said exuberantly, deliberately changing the subject.

"Your son is getting more like Big Brother every day," Rebecca said, still fuming.

"I have to admit he acts more like my father than my child," Sadie said, laughing. "But, he means well."

"I'm not kidding, Grandma. Sometimes he's just too much," she said, stabbing a chunk of lettuce with her fork.

When she heard a knock on the door, Sadie's mood shifted. Rebecca started to get up. Sadie placed her hand on Rebecca's shoulder. She knew who it was and thought it best if she answered. "No, sit down. I'll get it."

She grabbed her cane, hobbled to the door, looked though the peephole and opened it.

"I put it in my back pocket and forgot about it. I'm so sorry," Kurt said, handing her the key ring.

"It's a good thing Leon had a copy. Otherwise, I would have been locked out," she said sharply. "Anyway, you could have left it over at Jewish Seniors with David. You didn't have to come back here."

"I thought I should . . ."

Sadie's face turned red with anger. "Don't worry, you never have to come here again. I'm having you fired. I'm calling David."

"They can't fire me. I'm a volunteer, you crazy old . . ."

"Say it, why don't you just say it—crazy old Jew. Say it, you bastard," she shouted.

Rebecca rushed to her side. "Grandma, what's going on here? Who's this guy?"

Sadie composed herself. "Nobody," she said. "Everything's fine."

"Don't worry—I was just leaving," Kurt said. He turned around and stomped off.

Sadie slammed the door.

"Grandma, are you sure you're all right? What was that all about?" Rebecca said, wrapping her arm around Sadie's shoulders.

"I'm fine. It was just that *schmendrick* from Germany. I told you about him, remember?"

"He's that volunteer? He sure doesn't look the type."

"That's exactly what I thought when I met him. David should have his head examined."

Rebecca grabbed her jacket and handbag from the coatrack near the door. "I have to get back to school now, Grandma—Anatomy class in twenty minutes."

"Good. You can tell me about all the bones I've broken."

"You sure you're okay?"

"Yes already. Go on, don't be late. Anyway, I'm exhausted and I'm going to take a nap."

Rebecca raced down the hallway toward the elevator where she found Kurt banging on the down button. She watched him in silence. He must have sensed someone behind him and turned around. There was something about him that she found compelling, like those gorgeous, brooding men on the Calvin Klein billboards.

"Why did you give my grandmother such a hard time? She's almost ninety for God's sake and has a fractured arm and leg. Why did you yell her at like that?" she demanded.

"She gives me a hard time, too. She yelled, too."

"Clearly, you're not the apologizing type," she said and hurried toward the stairwell. Kurt followed her.

"I did nothing wrong," he said to the back of her head.

"My grandmother spent her teenage years in Auschwitz. Who'd you expect, Mary Poppins?" she said, as she sprinted down the steps with Kurt at her heels.

"I didn't know what to expect. I guess I wasn't prepared," he said, hurrying after her.

She stopped at the first floor landing, turned and studied his face, as if trying to measure his sincerity.

"Right—young Germans atoning for old sins. So how come you joined? You don't exactly look or act like the Good Samaritan type," she said, rushing down the last flight of stairs without waiting for an answer. She opened the stairway door with Kurt straggling behind her.

"You don't think I look saintly?" he said, dashing after her onto the street.

"That's not the word I would use to describe you," she said as they reached the bus stop.

"I needed to get out of Berlin and away from my parents."

"Now that I can relate to," Rebecca said.

"I have no idea why I am being so honest, I'm usually tight-lipped about myself, but here it is . . . my mother wants me to follow in my father's footsteps—delivering mail. My father wants me to join the army to make a man out of me. I'm not sure what I want to do with the rest of my life, but I know it's not that."

The bus arrived.

"And you got sent to boot camp anyway with my grandmother as your drill sergeant," she said with a grin and boarded.

*   *   *

Kurt watched the bus as it barreled down East Broadway. She was the beautiful girl in the graduation picture in Sadie's living room. He'd never met anyone quite like her before—so direct—no bullshit. He hoped he would see her again.

Chapter 14

Sadie sits on the dirty floor of a crowded barracks. Dozens of women look on as she uses old scraps of paper to wipe away the sweat streaming from a frail woman's face. The woman is lying on the lower level of a bunk bed and a younger girl sits beside Sadie, handing her the scraps of paper. The woman moans with pain.

"Shush, shush, they'll hear you," Sadie whispers.

The other women with gaunt faces beneath their butchered hair and frightened eyes crowd around Sadie, gaping at the fever-ridden woman. Their skeletal bodies huddle together around the bunk bed.

The frail woman coughs up blood that spurts all over Sadie and the younger girl, who tries to wipe the blood from her face with the scraps of paper that lie in a pile at her feet. The others gasp with horror and recoil at the sight of the blood pouring out of the frail woman's mouth.

A young Nazi guard with Kurt's face bursts into the barracks and glares at them. "Was geshiet, Frauleins?" he demands.

"Nothing, nothing . . . Gerty is very sick. She is burning up with fever. She needs a doctor," Sadie pleads.

"Verrückt Juden—she doesn't need a doctor, she needs this." He points his rifle at Gerty's head.

Sadie yells, "No. No. No. Don't!"

*   *   *

Sadie sat up slowly, grabbed some tissues from the nightstand, and wiped her face. Drenched like Gerty's, she thought. She took long, deep breaths and drank from a glass of water, laid her head back on the pillow, and struggled to erase the horrific images of the nightmare from her mind. This was the fifth in the last two weeks.

She looked over to the other side bed where Max used to sleep, remembering how they would take turns waking each other from the nightly reminders of their respective years in Auschwitz, screaming and sweating, grateful that they had each other to hold in their arms, then gently falling back to sleep, reminding each other that they were blessed to be in their soft, comfortable bed, safe and sound. The nightmares eventually subsided, recurring only once in awhile until now.

That was it. She would have to talk to David about getting someone else to assist her. Whatever this little *pisher's* intentions were, she could no longer bear being in his presence.

Chapter 15

David ushered Kurt into Noah's Ark, a brightly lit, crowded kosher restaurant on Grand Street. They stepped to the end of a long line of lunchtime patrons waiting to be seated. The tables were set with white linen table cloths, silver and china.

Kurt read a *New York Times* review posted by the entrance. "So this is the best kosher restaurant in New York City," he said to David. "How many other kosher restaurants are there?"

"About two hundred, if you include Brooklyn. We do have the largest Jewish population in the country," David said, smiling proudly.

The crowd included a mixture of young men and women casually dressed, young men wearing yarmulkes, older men wearing black hats trimmed with fur and ill-fitted black suits; their sideburns were long and curled. He had seen them many times before in the neighborhood, but wasn't sure who they were.

Kurt gestured to the men in the fur hats. "Who are those men? They look weird, like they're time travelers from the 1800s?"

"Hassidic Jews. Ultra orthodox and mystical. They believe that their faith separates them from other people. The side curls are called *payot*. Most people, including other Jews, think they're strange. They live by their own rules, kind of like a cult," David said as the line moved forward. "And, there are also Jews who are Conservative or Reform as well as Jews who are self-proclaimed Agnostics or Atheists or secular humanists."

Kurt never thought there were different types of Jews—he always assumed they were all alike. Different than Christians.

David had invited him to lunch to have a "talk", and he wasn't looking forward to this meal or another one of David's longwinded lectures. He wanted to get it over with, make their lunch brief, and maybe take a walk, figure out what to do next.

"Did Mrs. Seidenberg say anything to you about me?" he asked, direct and to the point.

He knew he'd crossed the line with Sadie.

David stared at him solemnly. "Yes, she did, but let's wait until we're seated so we can have a private conversation."

A stout, middle-aged woman wearing an excessive amount of eye makeup with one eyebrow higher than the other, as if she stepped out of a Picasso painting, led them to the back of the room. When they ultimately reached their table, the woman handed them oversized menus and, without a word, hobbled away.

Kurt was overwhelmed by the number of choices. He wasn't sure he'd like this Jewish food as he was nauseated by the distinctive odor of burnt chicken fat, which permeated the entire room.

David closed his menu and sniffed the air. "Doesn't it smell wonderful in here?"

"It smells like they cook with gallons of *schmalz*," Kurt said, on the verge of gagging.

"In Yiddish it's *Schmaltz* and yes they cook generously with it here. It's delicious and a very important ingredient in Ashkenazi Jewish cuisine. Have you heard of the Ashkenazi Jews?"

Kurt shook his head and braced himself for a lengthy speech on the subject—the man was like a walking encyclopedia.

"The Ashkenazi Jews are an ethnic division formed during the Holy Roman Empire, and they established communities throughout Central and Eastern Europe," David said, unfolding his napkin and smoothing it out on his lap. "They made a remarkable contribution to humanity and to all fields of endeavor, particularly to European culture."

A bald waiter dressed in a gold gabardine jacket and black trousers came over to the table and took their order, thankfully shortening David's tedious spiel. Kurt had never met anyone quite like David before—incessantly pontificating on a moment's notice.

"We'll have two orders of matzah ball soup, two orders of stuffed cabbages and two briskets with potato latkes," David said.

"What's matzah ball soup?" Kurt said when the waiter left, relieved that David ordered for the both of them, but dreading this meal.

"Matzah ball soup is just chicken broth with vegetables and balls made out of matzah meal. It's a Jewish classic," he said and then leaned in close, the expression on his face changed from neutral to concerned.

"Listen, Kurt, Sadie Seidenberg lodged a very serious complaint against you. She said you have no business helping Jews and that you should be sent back to Germany where you belong."

A busboy arrived a their table with two tall glasses of ice water and placed them on the table. David immediately grabbed a glass and took a sip. "Did you call her a crazy old Jew?"

"No, no, I never said that. She started it. She shouted at me first," Kurt said unevenly.

"The other volunteers from Project Remembrance have all been dedicated, compassionate young people. I don't know how you slipped by," David said, straightening the edges of his napkin.

Kurt shrugged. "I never thought about what would be expected of me when I joined. I didn't think I would meet someone as difficult as Sadie. The minute she laid eyes on me she had it in for me."

"You have a choice, you can either change your attitude immediately . . ."

"My attitude? What about hers?"

David dismissed his objections with a wave of his hand.

"Which includes making amends with Mrs. Seidenberg, or I'm going to have to report that your work here is totally unsatisfactory and recommend that your organization ship you back to Berlin. I'll give you one week to shape up. I think that's more than fair. Don't you?"

Kurt bowed his head and nodded. He knew something like this would happen.

The waiter arrived with their soups and *challah* bread.

"Here we have real kosher cooking even my own grandmother would be proud to serve," David said, shifting back to being the Jewish culinary tour guide.

Kurt dipped his spoon into the soup and sampled it. The soup journeyed down his throat and landed in his stomach and lay there like a huge blob of gum.

"It has more flavor than my mother's," he said. No need to insult the food. Even he knew better than that. He was in enough trouble as it was. In truth, this was no compliment, his mother's cooking was awful—everything was either burnt or tasted like cardboard. He had to play along.

Above all, he did not want to be sent back to Germany.

He nudged the two beige, oval shaped balls floating in the bowl. "Are these dumplings?" he asked.

"They're matzah balls. Try one. Break off a small piece with your spoon and taste it. I guarantee it won't kill you."

David watched as he nibbled at the soft, mushy ball devoid of any flavor.

"So, what's the verdict?" David said.

"Well, it's kind of bland, but it's also kind of tangy. I can taste the chicken fat in them," Kurt said, understating the obvious.

"The food here is good whether you like it or not. What about Sadie Seidenberg—are you in or are you out?"

Chapter 16

Kurt whispered into the pay phone in the YMHA lobby in a futile attempt to be unheard by Tony, who stood directly behind him, waiting his turn.

"Karin, pick up for Christ sakes. Are you there? Call me back. *Verdammt.*" He slammed the receiver into its cradle so hard it rattled.

"Women," Tony said. "They're never there when you need them. Am I right or am I right?"

"She doesn't even return my calls or emails anymore."

"You never know with women. One day they don't want you, the next day they want you back. Usually when they see you. Otherwise, it's out of sight out of mind," Tony said, patting him on his shoulder.

Kurt stood in front of Karin's building and glanced up at her bedroom window. A dim light flickered. She wouldn't leave a candle burning if she wasn't home. He'd never returned her building key and entered. He rushed up the six flights of stairs, knocked and waited, catching his breath. After a moment, he knocked again.

Karin opened the door, but left the chain on. "Are you crazy?" she said in a low voice, obviously annoyed. "Why didn't you call first?"

"I did, I just called you. You never answer your damn phone and you don't return my calls. Can I come in?"

"No, Kurt. I'm not alone."

Her red silk Chinese brocaded kimono revealed a peek of her bare breasts and legs. It was as if she intentionally left it loosely fastened. It infuriated him.

"That's the robe I bought you last Christmas. I skipped lunches for a whole month to save enough money and now you're wearing it for another man."

"You want it back?" she said.

"I'm having a very hard time here now, Karin. I got in trouble with the Jews. I need you."

"Grow up, Kurt. You can deal with this yourself. I'm not your fucking mother," she said, shutting the door in his face.

He stood fixated on the door and leaned against it. He then lumbered down the stairs and thought about drowning his sorrows on authentic German beer at his favorite bar, Zum Schnieder, a pretty close replica of an indoor beer garden on Avenue C. It reminded him of Berlin. He'd go there when he was feeling particularly homesick, sometimes with Karin and sometimes not. He decided against it as it would probably depress him even more. All he really wanted to do was to go back to his temporary jail cell and wallow.

He walked over to the bus stop and caught the bus uptown. He rested his head against the bus window and watched the streets zip by, wondering why the fuck she was so heartless. *How could she just discard him like a pair of old shoes that were no longer in style?*

When the bus stopped at 93rd Street, he hopped off and trudged past Sal's Italian Kitchen, his favorite pizza place a block away from the Y. He smelled the rich aroma of Italian spices and thought about grabbing a couple slices, his usual dinner, but he wasn't really hungry.

Kurt, overwhelmed by Karin's callousness, slogged into the YMHA lobby, sneaked past the front desk, his head down, his spirit broken.

"Hey, man, Kurt. Kurt?" Tony said, practicing a lick on his unplugged guitar. How he envied Tony. His music was his passion. He spent every moment he could, day and night, devoted to becoming a better guitar player, the next Eric Clapton or Jimi Hendrix. His art was once his passion, his obsession. He couldn't imagine ever feeling that way again.

Although he just wanted to go upstairs and sulk alone, he went over to the desk anyway.

"You look like shit," Tony said.

"Fucking Karin was screwing somebody," he said.

He felt Tony looking at him as if waiting for the right words to come to him. They didn't. "I'm going to jam in a club in the West Village later," Tony mumbled. "There'll be mucho senoritas."

"I'm done with women. I'm too fucked up."

"That's perfect. Women love guys when they're fucked up. It's their nurturing instinct," Tony said and stopped plucking. "Hey, at least you have your work, right?"

Kurt headed toward the elevators. He'd kill himself, but he was too much of a coward.

In his room, he gazed at the framed but now glassless photograph of Karin on his bureau. He hadn't had the heart to throw it out. He ripped it out of the frame, crumpled it into a ball, aimed it at the wastebasket under his desk, but missed. While picking it up and dropping it in the trash, he noticed the stack of booklets on Judaism sitting idly on his desk, that David gave him at his first day orientation.

Kurt gazed at the title of the top booklet *An Introduction to Jewish Belief.* He'd only read the first five pages. He sat down, opened it up and began to read. Maybe if he knew more about the Jews, it would seem as if he was making an effort.

Chapter 17

Kurt waited for the downtown bus, silently reciting various versions of apologies for Sadie. He hadn't asked for forgiveness since he was a child. He remembered once his father had demanded him to apologize to his mother for breaking her antique beer stein. It had a ceramic blue and white base with a pewter lid and had the Prince of Pilsen etched in the center. Her father had given it to her for a wedding present and it had been in his family for many generations. It was ancient and supposed to be worth a small fortune. When Kurt was nine, he had knocked his soccer ball into the small round table in the parlor where the stein was on display, shattering it to pieces. He didn't think it was his fault; it was just an accident. He apologized, but his father said it wasn't loud or sincere enough and beat his bottom with a strap until Kurt shouted what his father considered a heartfelt apology, tears streaming down his face.

He stepped off the bus and traipsed over to the housing projects, imagining the worst. Would she slap him on sight or yell at him like the last time—or maybe she would refuse to speak to him and demand he go back to David and get another assignment.

He entered the building and got in the elevator, narrowly escaping being run down by a bunch of kids who were getting off. All the buttons had been pressed, consequently the elevator stopped on every floor, giving him more time to dread his upcoming confrontation with Sadie and to practice his apology.

He got off on the sixth floor, walked to Sadie's door and knocked. He heard a whisper, "Who's there?"

The voice was definitely not Sadie's, it was higher pitched. He was pretty sure it was Rebecca. How fortunate for him as she had wandered in and out of his thoughts since they met. He gladly identified himself.

Rebecca opened the door, peering skeptically past the chain. Kurt smiled politely, practically demurely, barely able to conceal his joy. He was thrilled to see her.

"Can I speak with your grandmother, please?"

"What do you want with her?" she asked, staring at him warily, as if she'd already formed an opinion of him and it wasn't favorable. Oh no, bad sign. Perhaps he should have said hello first, made some small talk, behaved neighborly. Might as well come out with it.

"I want to make peace with her," he said, stammering, his anxiety getting the better of him.

"Oh, now you want to negotiate a ceasefire instead of prolonging your conflict or waging another battle," Rebecca said, sounding practical, like a much older woman would. That was the thing about girls, and it certainly was with Karin. One moment they sounded like sages, the next like little babies.

He waited while Rebecca released the chain, opened the door wider and, stepping out into the hallway, forcing him to move back. "Well, she's asleep now, so you'll have to come back another time or you could just call her up."

"David thought I should apologize to her in person," he said, knowing immediately after the words tumbled out of his mouth it was the wrong thing to say and that she'd be even more pissed at him than she was before.

"So David told you to do this. You didn't think it was necessary to make peace with my grandmother yourself after the way you treated her. She was very upset, you know," Rebecca said, raising her voice.

She stepped back to the doorway, tilted her ear inside the apartment seemingly to hear if she'd awakened Sadie and once she determined she hadn't, walked farther into the hallway and closed the door behind her. She cocked her head to one side, accentuating her anger, and glared at him.

"I'm sorry, really I am. I've been having such a hard time here," he said, hoping she'd understand what he was going through. "I thought I would be with other volunteers and make new friends, but it's just me and David and he's not that easy to get along with. He seems disappointed in me and is constantly comparing me to Wolfgang, the previous volunteer."

She stared at him for a moment. "I don't think she's quite ready to bury the hatchet just yet," she said. "You need to give her more time."

"Maybe you can tell me what to say—how to talk to her. I'm not sure I know. I need a translator or something. I always say the wrong thing," he said in the most pathetic voice he could muster and actually felt that way.

"That's obvious. I guess elderly Jewish-ese is hard to master. I could help you, though I'm not sure why or even if I can."

"When? I mean, when would be a good time?" he said.

"I don't know, Kurt," she said and he was delighted to hear that she remembered his name.

"If you want me to beg a little more, I would gladly do it," he said and meant it.

She leaned in to him a little as if plotting a conspiracy.

"I can't promise you anything, I'm pretty busy with school these days, but I'll get in touch with you as soon as possible," she said and stepped back toward the door.

"Oh, please, if you can, and thank you. Thank you so much, You can reach me at Jewish Seniors or the 92nd Street Y," he said, fearing that he'd thanked her too much.

"Okay," Rebecca said with a curious look on her face, appearing as if she was mulling over their interaction in her mind. She then flashed a courteous smile, turned around, walked into the apartment and closed the door without once looking back.

Maybe his situation wasn't as hopeless as it seemed. He was sure that, being as intelligent as she was, she would weigh the pros and cons. Something about Rebecca made him feel that if she said she'd do something, she'd actually do it.

Chapter 18

Kurt sat across from a very solemn David whose face was pale, ghost-like. Glancing around the Jewish Senior's office, Kurt noticed that others also had the life drained from their faces.

"A very terrible thing happened last night," he said, his voice quivering. He placed his hand on Kurt's arm. "Rabbi Feldman's synagogue was vandalized last night, inside and out."

It took a moment for Kurt to register what David had said. These things only happened in the past, in his grandfather's time.

"Who would do such a thing? Was anyone there?" Kurt said.

David stared at him somberly. "The synagogue was empty. No one was hurt. Who did it? Who knows? Unfortunately, we have neo-Nazi groups here in New York and they have been more active since 9-11. Jews always get blamed for everything. Anti-Semites think Israel was responsible," David said, opening a manila folder on his desk and scanning the document inside. "It says here in your file that you went to an arts university in Berlin for two years. We're in desperate need of an artist now. The vandals defaced every wall, inside and out, including the mural. You'll see for yourself when you go to the synagogue."

Kurt had forgotten that Karin had put down that he attended the

Berlin University of the Arts on his Project Remembrance application. He'd preferred to omit it, but Karin insisted that he had to ac-
count for those years after high school.

"I'm not sure I can do that," he said. The thought of returning to
painting knocked the wind out of him.

"What's the problem? You're an artist—that's what it says in your
profile. I Googled your school and it's very prestigious. I read that the
selection process for its students is highly competitive and that the
applicants come from all over the world. If you were accepted, your
work must be superior."

"But, I haven't painted anything for over a year," he said, squirm-
ing. "Much less a mural."

"I'm sure you'll be a hundred times better than anyone else, given
the synagogue's available funds, which is zilch."

Half an hour later, Kurt ambled toward the synagogue; he was in no
rush to get there. What a way to get back into painting—saddled with
the overwhelming task of restoring a Jewish church.

He remembered the pictures of the devastation during *Kristallnacht* he saw as a child in grammar school—smashed temples ruined
beyond recognition. Shattered store windows and façades defaced
with anti-Jewish slogans. Some shops were set on fire. He wasn't sure
what he would see at Rabbi Feldman's synagogue. David's description
of the vandalism was vague.

He braced himself as he neared. Red paint dripped like blood all
over the once beautiful exterior with the words *All Jews Must Die* and
Burn Dirty Jews scrawled in red over it.

Why the fuck did this have to happen now, as if Sadie didn't hate
him enough. This destruction could only make matters worse for him.
Fuck!

Several police cars were parked in front; yellow crime scene tape was strung over large orange cones on each side of the entrance. He focused on the two large wooden doors with the intricately engraved Stars of David on each panel he admired just a short while ago. They were now covered with painted red swastikas. He gaped at the Nazi symbols. He'd read in one of his art books that swastikas were once used as decorative good luck symbols dating back to ancient India. The swastika was even a sacred icon in Hinduism, Buddhism and many other religions. Hard to believe, now that it's branded all over the Western world as a trademark of hate and violence, and outlawed in Germany.

The magnificent stone sculptured doorframe was swathed in red paint. How was all of this going to be repaired? It's going to take an army of men to undo this amount of damage.

Kurt went inside and took in the vandals' handiwork in the lobby—it, too, was covered in red swastikas and hateful Anti-Semitic slogans: *Death to all Jews; Hitler was right*. The last time he saw so many swastikas in one place was when he watched old footage of Nazi rallies from 1933 in his high school history class. He recalled how astonished he was that so many Germans succumbed to Hitler's psychosis, his maniacal plans that would almost destroy Germany. How the fuck did that happen? He couldn't imagine it ever happening again.

He then ambled inside the interior and studied the mural and the surrounding walls and it was defaced with even more swastikas and slogans. Sections of the beautiful mural was smeared in red—what was once a magnificent piece of religious art was now a sacrilegious disaster.

He couldn't believe that the horror of Nazism that he saw in his grammar and high school textbooks and documentaries in Germany was replicated here now in a small synagogue in New York City. How the fuck would he alone repair it? There were artists that specialized in restoring religious paintings, but he was not one of them.

Several people wearing jackets that said CSI on the back and latex gloves were dusting the walls and seats for fingerprints. He knew those letters from the American television series, *CSI,* crime scene investigators. Others searched the floor with flashlights for evidence—clothing threads, strands of hair—and placed them into plastic bags and hoped that they would find clues that would lead to the capture of the culprits. Good luck to them. Many people came in and out of this building; to find strands of hair matching to a criminal was going to take a miracle. Did Jews believe in miracles? He had a sudden desire to turn around and run away.

It had occurred to him that, as a German, he could possibly be thought of as a suspect.

He observed Rabbi Feldman, who looked obviously distressed, talking with a young uniformed policeman and another man in his mid-forties, dressed in a weathered suit, who was probably one of those plainclothes detectives, an accurate description of what this man was wearing.

As Kurt stepped toward them, the detective turned to the rabbi and gestured toward Kurt. "Who's this?" he said.

"He must be Kurt Lichter, my volunteer. I'm expecting him."

"If you say so, Rabbi. We'll be in touch," the detective said, sizing Kurt up.

Relieved, he watched the detective and the policeman leave the synagogue, although he was almost certain they couldn't arrest him for being German and dressed like a biker.

Rabbi Feldman gaped at the mutilated mural. "Thank you for coming and helping us here, Kurt."

Awkwardly, he turned to the rabbi. "It's terrible. In Germany they do this to mosques now."

"So what else is new?" the rabbi said and paused for a moment. "I have to tell you how relieved I am that we have an artist helping us here. It's a big task, but a good one. David told me that you attended one of Europe's finest art universities."

Kurt could feel his face burning up. The last thing he needed now was this kind of pressure. These people were actually counting on him. Shit!

Rabbi Feldman sat down in the first row and gestured for Kurt to sit next to him. "I'm sorry but I don't know where to tell you to start. It's so overwhelming. We have a small congregation here and a few of them are Holocaust survivors so I think the sooner the better, if it's at all possible," he said, clasping his hands. "I don't want them to fall back into the deep depression and paranoia they experienced after the war. It's been all over the news—on TV and radio programs and all of the newspapers including *The Jewish Daily Forward*, which I know many of my survivors read."

"It's such a shame . . . I'm so sorry," Kurt said, not knowing what else to say.

"You don't have to be. It's not your fault. But, if it makes you feel any better I accept your apology," the rabbi said and paused for a moment. "I guess the best thing to do is to start with the lobby first. We'll need primer, white paint, brushes and rollers. There's a hardware store a couple of blocks away. Why don't we stock up on all the supplies today and get an early start tomorrow morning? We can start with the interior walls and then the mural. First things first."

Chapter 19

Kurt reached up in his closet, took down his wooden paint box and set it on his bed. He wiped the dust off with the edge of his tee shirt and opened it. He stared at the contents: brushes of various sizes, oil paint tubes, turpentine and rags all in pitiable condition. He picked up the brushes and inspected them, running his fingers over the stiff bristles, a few still had remnants of old oil paint. He was never good at taking care of them properly. He checked his paint tubes. Some of them were rusted and unusable, but there were others that were salvageable. Would his worn brushes and used oil paints be up to the job ahead of him? Would he?

He placed his supplies back in the box and carried it out of his room to the communal bathroom a few feet away. Several young men were primping in front of the mirror that stretched along the length of the wall, getting ready for a night out.

These were his bathroom buddies; they never exchanged more than nods, smiles and polite conversation, which they did now. There was one guy who ran his fingers, drenched in gel, through his hair over and over again to perfect a tousled look. He paused a moment to give Kurt a quick salute, which was his way of saying hello. Kurt had learned that he and his cronies were once soldiers in the Israeli army and were now in New York to continue their studies.

He wished his life was as simple as theirs, that he was free to do whatever he wanted to do instead of being at David's beck and call.

Kurt opened the box, removed the contents and brought them to the sink. First, he ran the hot water over the brush heads, squirting liquid soap all over them as he had when he was in school. He rubbed them continuously until the sable bristles softened. Tiny clumps of paint remained in a couple of the twelve-, ten- and nine-inch brushes. He then saturated those brushes with what was left in his bottle of Motsenbocker's oil paint remover, vigorously rubbing the heads with a rag, emitting a distinct odor. Kurt hadn't remembered that happening before. Maybe because the last time he used it was over a year ago.

The gel-fingered man next him scrunched up his nose. "What's that? It smells like rotten eggs in here. Are you trying to kill us?"

His compatriots echoed his sentiments. "Can't you wait until we're finished?" said the man washing his hands to the left of him.

He apologized and told them that he had nowhere else to go. He explained about his task at the synagogue thinking they would empathize with him. After all, he was restoring a synagogue's mural.

He could still hear them protesting vociferously as they cleared out into the hallway. Kurt noticed on a few occasions that these Israelis had hair-trigger tempers and would go off on each other for no real reason in particular.

He checked the tubes of paint to see which ones were still fit for use. Some were completely dried out and rusted, others were surprisingly still fresh. He made a mental note of the additional colors he would need to tackle the mural, and dumped the unusable ones in the trash.

He had studied Renaissance painting his first year at the university and received positive feedback on his work. He now would have to channel that knowledge in order to repair his status among the Jews and not be deported back to Berlin in disgrace. He imagined his mother's voice lamenting about the shame he had brought upon his family once again and his father shouting: "Can't you do anything right for once in your life?"

Kurt woke up the next morning dreading the seemingly insurmountable job ahead of him at Rabbi Feldman's damaged synagogue. First he had to deal with nasty, spiteful Sadie Seidenberg and now this.

At the synagogue, a crowd of people—old, young, black, brown and white—silently observed two workmen wearing white jumpsuits with large goggles over their eyes as they stood on a scaffold scraping the blood red swastikas and vile words off the exterior of the building with large wire brushes. All eyes were riveted, as if they were in a movie theater watching an edge of your seat suspense thriller.

Kurt watched as clumps of red paint fell to the ground, exposing the ultra faded brick. Another workman on a tall ladder, using a steel wood pad, rubbed the stone sculptured doorframe, removing the bright red paint.

He stared at the large wooden doors that appeared to be sanded down. The two large red swastikas that obscured the engraved Stars of David were thankfully no longer there. He assumed that the doors would eventually be stained dark mahogany, their original color, and felt relieved that the restoration had begun so vigorously.

At least he wasn't the only one responsible for the enormous task ahead of them.

Kurt tried opening the door, but it was locked. Kurt knocked and waited. After a few minutes, Rabbi Feldman opened the chained door.

"Do you believe this? A secured house of worship. Now it's more like a fortress," the rabbi said, releasing the chain and ushering Kurt inside. "The police asked me keep the door locked as an extra precaution. They even have a patrol car checking this street every so often."

Part of the back wall in the lobby had been painted over, only the words *Hitler Was Right* and a large red swastika remained. A ladder was left standing with a roller and paint tray.

"A couple of young men from the congregation were here last night," the rabbi said. "They made a good start. Why don't you continue here with the roller?"

He handed Kurt some pictures. "I found these photographs of the mural when it was first painted in 1902 and some later photos in an old file cabinet in my office. I don't know how much help they'll be, since they're so aged."

Kurt looked through the pile of pictures, some were black and white—yellowed, faded, barely legible and obviously taken at a distance; others were in color, but were wedding or Bar Mitzvah photos posed in front of a single section. "It's better than nothing . . . I guess," he said. "I think I remember some of the original colors from when I was here with Mrs. Seidenberg."

Kurt set his paint box down on the floor, he wouldn't be needing it just yet. He eyed the remainder of the defaced lobby, wondering how many coats it would take to cover the numerous red swastikas and blasphemous words on the walls.

The rabbi started to leave but abruptly turned back and called out Kurt's name.

"Yes, rabbi," he said, turning around to face him.

He walked over to Kurt and shook his hand. "Thank you. Thank you again for your help. We couldn't do this without you."

Uneasy with the rabbi's gratitude, Kurt nodded stiffly. "I'll try to do the best I can," he said. He had no other choice.

He watched the rabbi as he headed back to his office, surprised that the rabbi actually trusted him with this enormous responsibility. He'd never experienced this feeling before. Someone was actually depending on him to do something that was really important to them.

He moved the ladder to the still vandalized section of the lobby and climbed. He poured the white paint into the tray, firmly gripped the roller and dipped it into the paint. He pressed it over the words, *Hitler was right*. He rolled over the words several times, applying as much pressure on the roller as possible, as if he alone could eradicate anti-Semitism, but the red still bled through. He continued to bear down over and over again until the words finally vanished.

He then climbed down and moved the ladder directly in front of a large red swastika, ascended and again pressed the roller against it, rolling it back and forth, until it disappeared and that section of the wall was once again clean and white. He felt a sense of deep satisfaction. But, there was a lot more work to be done.

Chapter 20

Kurt raced toward the NYU Medical Center front entrance and spotted Rebecca standing on the sidewalk.

She wore a charcoal gray down parka with the faux fur trimmed hood partially covering her striking wavy, reddish brown hair. Karin would never hide her long, sleek, straight blonde hair with a hood or hat; it was her best feature. Rebecca was a couple of inches shorter and didn't have that gorgeous, supermodel look that Karin had, but her natural, shining beauty was definitely Karin's equivalent.

"I'm so sorry I'm late. I only just got your message," he said as he rushed up to her. He was still wearing his paint-splattered clothes and hoped she wouldn't mention his appearance.

"So you paint houses in your spare time?" she said, checking him over.

"I didn't have time to change. I was helping repair Rabbi Feldman's synagogue," he said.

"Oh God. I heard about it on the news. I haven't mentioned it to my grandmother. I'm afraid to. But she follow the news, so I'm sure she's heard about it."

"Yes, it's terrible, such destruction everywhere," he said, zippering up his jacket, hiding a white smudge on his black tee shirt. "I'm so glad you decided to see me."

"I have to be back in thirty minutes, but do you want to grab a cup of coffee? There's a Starbucks on the corner," she said, steering him toward it.

"Do they have Starbucks in Berlin?" she added.

"Oh yes, there are many. I used to go to the one on Kurfuerstendamn Boulevard with my girl . . . my ex-girlfriend," Kurt said, relieved that he corrected his eligibility status.

"It's a worldwide epidemic. There's no escape," she said, grinning.

"Scientists all over the world must be trying to find the antidote to cure the need for trendy drinks," Kurt said, hoping his retort was clever enough.

Although this was not officially a date, he felt the tension between them. It was too soon for that. She was here to advise him, to mend the broken fence with Sadie. Nonetheless, he experienced a tingling sensation in his stomach and couldn't help flirting a little, not enough to be obnoxious, he hoped.

They waited on a short line. Kurt ordered an espresso and Rebecca a tall latte. He wanted to pay for her drink, but had barely enough to buy his. Luckily, she beat him to it and paid for her own.

She directed him to a table in a corner. Rebecca removed her down jacket, draped it over the back of her chair while he swirled his coffee with a wooden stir stick. He noticed her forehead had tightened, forming lines above her wide eyes. Kurt sensed she was gathering her thoughts. And he was right.

"You have to be the one to give a little, to give more," she said. "Neither you nor I can have any idea what life was like in a concentration camp, not knowing if you will live or die one moment to the next. Not knowing what sort of atrocity will be visited upon you.

Witnessing horrors being perpetrated on the people around you. Feeling so completely powerless, imprisoned, although you have not committed a crime, and you're only sixteen years old."

"I know," said Kurt.

"Do you really? You're the one that has to make allowances for my grandmother, for her age and history. Not the other way around."

"I tried," Kurt said, dabbing his mouth with his napkin.

"No you didn't. I saw your face, heard your tone."

"But . . ."

"No buts. You wanted me to help you, so here's my advice. You have to stop being mad at your job here and just do it unselfishly. You volunteered for this work. You weren't forced into it," she said, her eyes fixed on his.

He felt beads of perspiration on the back of his neck and slipped off his jacket. He wasn't prepared for her directness. All the flirtation was drained from the conversation, from the very room.

"Yes, I did volunteer, but it's because I wanted to come to New York. I didn't feel a responsibility to atone for my grandparents' sins. That happened over seventy years ago and I hadn't even thought about the Holocaust since grade school, when we were taught briefly about it," he said, wondering if she had slipped sodium pentothal into his drink. He hadn't intended on being this honest.

"My grandmother never spoke to me about it," Rebecca said. "Once, when I was six, she and my grandfather stayed at our house for a couple of weeks and I walked in on her in the bathroom. She was in a sleeveless nightgown and I saw the numbers tattooed on her arm. When I asked her what they were, she turned red and trembled. I got scared and ran out of the bathroom. I asked my mother about them and she said it had to do with the war, but I must never ask my grandmother about it again." She sipped her latte. "When I was older my father told me that grandma was in Auschwitz. He said that was all he knew. She never talked about those years. As you can imagine, it's not a popular topic at family gatherings."

Kurt stared at her pensively. Auschwitz, that wasn't even in Germany. If he remembered correctly, it was in Poland, but he suspected she probably already knew that and decided to keep this information to himself. Anyway, it was the Germans that built that camp and not the Poles. He couldn't remember the last time he had a serious conversation like this with Karin.

"What should I do now? How can I make peace with her?" he said, leaning forward, looking intently into her eyes.

Rebecca blushed, seemingly embarrassed by his gaze. "Apologize to her, but do it because you want to, because you sincerely, in your heart, want to help her. Be patient, listen and don't challenge her," she said, checking her watch. "Oh, God, I have a class in ten minutes."

She stood and put her jacket on. "She has to go to the doctor next week to get the cast taken off her arm. I'll be taking exams, so I could suggest that you take her."

Kurt stood up and thanked her. "Maybe we could talk again sometime, if you want."

"Maybe," she said.

He watched her walk away and even though she was a bit harsh with him, the way she said "maybe" made him feel like there was some hope there. After all, she didn't say "no."

Chapter 21

Sadie sat in her brocaded burgundy wingback chair and proudly watched Rebecca making her bed, paying a good deal of attention to the hospital corners.

"Did your mother, may she rest in peace, teach you that?"

"No, actually, it was my father. The same way you taught him."

Sadie laughed, remembering. "So stubborn. He wanted to do everything himself," she said, staring at a picture on her dresser of Jack as a child, dressed as a cowboy. "There he is, the big *macher,* when he was seven," Sadie said, pointing to the picture. "He begged your grandfather, may he rest in peace, for a whole month to buy him that outfit."

"I can't imagine him ever being a child," Rebecca said, throwing a slightly faded burgundy and beige flowered comforter over the sheets. She smoothed the wrinkles, turned down one corner, helped Sadie into the bed and sat beside her.

"Grandma, how did you meet grandpa? You never told me."

Sadie looked at Max's picture that was next to the cowboy Jack photo. He was dressed in a loosely fitted dark suit with a white shirt and dark tie and wore one of those '40's fedoras that looked too large for his head. His smile was weak and his eyes were half-closed. He hated having his picture taken.

"Oh, it was a lifetime ago, just after the war. It's a long story, sweetheart. Too long. Not now, maybe another time I'll tell you about it," Sadie said, sighing.

"Do you want a cup of chamomile tea before I go?"

Sadie nodded. "That would be nice, if you have the time."

"My next class is in an hour, I have the time. I'll go and make your tea," she said as she left the room.

Sadie stared at her husband Max's picture remembering when she met him. Oh my . . . what a time it was—in a refugee camp in Poland after the camps had been liberated. There they were: two bald sickly skeletons around the same age, wearing dirty, tattered, smelly, striped clothing. Two survivors, both suffering from starvation and exhaustion, staring at each other with glazed, terrified eyes. Not knowing what was going to happen next. Where would they go? What would they do now? Their families were all murdered by the Nazis. Would they be able to pick up the pieces of their shattered lives? They gravitated toward each other as if the other was their savior and clung onto one another until the day he died. That was how she and the love of her life met. How could she begin to tell her granddaughter that story? She couldn't.

Rebecca came back into the room smiling, handed her the cup of tea and sat in the wingback chair.

"Soon you'll have your arm back again," Rebecca said.

Sadie sipped her tea and shook herself out of her past. "If I could have my leg back too—that I would like."

Rebecca asked when the cast was coming off, then told her about her exams and suggested that Kurt go with her.

"You remembered his name? I thought they fired him," Sadie said. Just hearing that impudent German boy's name enraged her.

"He's not as bad as you think, Grandma. He's helping repair the synagogue."

Sadie shuddered. "Oh my God, my synagogue—what a horrible thing. I had to shut off my television when I saw it on the news. I've been too terrified to go. What's he doing there?"

"He's an artist, Grandma. He's restoring the walls and the mural," Rebecca said, gently squeezing her grandmother's hand.

"An artist? What does that little *pisher* know about Jewish art?" Sadie said, narrowing her eyes. "How do you know all these things?"

"I ran into him . . . we had coffee," Rebecca said, careful to avoid her grandmother's eyes. But when she looked back, she found exactly what she'd expected—two dark glowing orbs, Sadie's bullshit detectors.

"Ran into him? You had coffee with him?" Sadie said, containing her anger when she noticed her granddaughter's frightened face.

"Grandma, we had a cup of coffee. Underneath all that leather, he's really an okay guy."

"Underneath all that leather, he's a *mamser* and don't you forget that."

"Don't most people deserve a second chance?" Rebecca said, kissing her grandmother's forehead.

Sadie didn't believe for one minute that Rebecca just ran into him. They would've had to have planned it. New York was a big city with over eight million people. And what would they have in common? Her sweet granddaughter with that nasty German boy. Her son would have a fit, if he found out. He would put an end to that relationship in a heartbeat.

Chapter 22

Kurt surveyed the interior of the synagogue, the back and front walls were once again white—no traces of the destruction. It was now time to tackle what he feared most—the mural. How the fuck was he ever going to recreate what was once beautifully depicted scenes from the Old Testament, now marred and bloodied, all by himself? His eyes scanned each section one by one and decided to tackle first the one that was least vandalized.

Kurt moved the ladder, with his paint box sitting on its shelf, in front of Moses leading the Hebrews out of Egypt. He climbed up, studied it, removed his palette knife from his paint box, and then began to scrape the hardened, red paint drippings off of the desert sands. The residue poured down over his face, shirt and pants, showering him with red dust particles as if he were caught in a sandstorm.

After wiping the red bits off his face and hair with a rag, he stared at what was left—blankness where the grains of sands once were. He closed his eyes and tried to imagine what colors were originally used to create the sands the Jews treaded through to reach their homeland. He recalled a technique he learned his second year at the arts university of using short brush strokes to create texture—one color next to the other.

He began by dipping his brush first in yellow, then dipped another brush in brown, then beige, transforming it into a mixture of all three colors, repeating the three colors continuously.

Rabbi Feldman spoke his name as he stepped under the ladder. Kurt completed his brush stroke and looked down.

"The sand looks so realistic—almost three dimensional," the rabbi said.

"I can hardly remember what those other sections looked like before," Kurt said, gesturing to Moses and the burning bush and Moses receiving the Ten Commandments on Mt. Sinai that were covered with dripping red paint. "There wasn't any clear photos of those sections."

"You could probably use some help," Rabbi Feldamn said, gazing at the mural.

"I thought there wasn't anyone else."

"I might know someone—it's a long shot. Oh and David wants you to call him right away. He needs you to do something for him. You can use the phone in my office," the rabbi said, steadying the ladder for Kurt to descend.

Kurt set down his brush, climbed down and walked over to the first row and put on his jacket, wondering what was so urgent that required him dropping his work at the synagogue.

"For such a young man you do a lot of worrying," the rabbi said, smiling.

"It's because everything in my life has gone exactly the opposite of the way I hoped it would. I'm not what you call a lucky person," Kurt said.

Chapter 23

Sadie sat as far away from Kurt as possible in the taxi and watched the passing streets. The cab was heavy with silence. She hadn't ever wanted to see him again, but she was concerned about his meeting with Rebecca and was about to speak when Kurt spoke first.

"Mrs. Seidenberg, I want to tell you how sorry I am for the way I behaved that last time I saw you," Kurt said. "I guess I'm having a hard time adjusting to my new life here. I know I was completely out of line. I'm so sorry."

She took a hard look at him. The thought of Rebecca and this German boy together enraged her. "You saw my granddaughter?" Sadie said.

"Yes . . . we had a cup of coffee," he said.

"She told me."

"She's a very nice girl."

"She's an angel. And she doesn't date boys like you," she said, raising her voice.

"Oh no, there was no date. We only had a cup of coffee."

"A regular coffee klatch," she said. "All right, so that's all it was. Just know that's all it will ever be."

Sadie's eyes narrowed as if she didn't believe a word he said. "Rebecca asked me to give you another chance. Is that why you had coffee with her?"

"No. I never asked her to say anything to you about me," he said.

"Second chance, second schmance. Just don't get any ideas about my Rebecca. You're not fit to walk the ground she stands on."

Kurt turned away from her, unzipped his jacket and rolled down his window. He needed some fresh air to cool off the heat generated by this conversation. Why was she being so cruel to him? He said he was sorry—what more did she want?

The cab pulled up to a doctor's entrance on the outside of a tall pre-World War Two apartment building on Manhattan's Upper East Side. Sadie paid the driver and Kurt got out and rushed over to help her.

"Don't bother, I can do it myself," she said, but she couldn't, so he picked up her cane from the floor, handed it to her and eased her onto the sidewalk. He tried to take her hand but she pulled it away.

The large, plain waiting room was filled with other patients with casts on their arms or legs or braces around their necks. Kurt tried to guide her into a seat at the end of a short, gray sofa, but she refused his help and tottered to a straight-backed, black leather chair on the other side of the room that looked extremely uncomfortable.

Kurt sat on the sofa and flipped through last month's *Architectural Digest* on the coffee table. A nurse holding a manila folder called out Sadie's name. Sadie tried to stand up by herself, but couldn't. Kurt hurried across the room and escorted her to the nurse, then returned to an article about a multi-million dollar beach house renovation in East Hampton, but he couldn't concentrate. Instead, he obsessed about what Sadie had said. Rebecca. It's true that Rebecca turned him on, she was so beautiful, honest and sincere, a terrific combination in a woman. But he'd been in love with Karin for so long, he couldn't remember a time when he wasn't crazy about her. It seemed odd to imagine feeling that way about another girl. Yet, Karin callously dumped him like a bag of trash, without giving it a second thought. Maybe it was time for someone else.

A half-hour later, the nurse guided Sadie into the waiting room. The cast had been removed, but her arm was still in the black cloth sling.

"How are you feeling now, Mrs. Seidenberg?" Kurt said as he went over to her.

"How do you think I feel? My arm is still in a sling and I'm still hobbling around with my cane and my one good leg."

"But at least your cast is off. Progress . . . yes?" he said, waiting for a response, but there was none.

He led her into the street and hailed a cab. He helped her in, and for the second time that day, she slid over to stare out of the opposite window. Again, they sat in silence.

When they reached the projects, she paid the fare, and he walked her to the entrance.

"You can go now. I'll be all right from here," Sadie said.

He pushed the door open and held it for her and she toddled inside. "I said I'll be fine from here," she repeated.

Kurt closed the door and made his way toward the uptown bus stop. He couldn't imagine that there was anything he could possibly do to improve his relationship with Sadie. It was beyond repair.

The bus veered toward the curb, and Kurt raced to catch up with it.

*   *   *

Sadie entered her apartment in a fury, her cane almost puncturing the floor. She went into the kitchen, grabbed the receiver from the wall phone and punched in numbers with a vengeance. "Mr. Seidenberg, please. It's his mother."

She and Jack went through the usual pleasantries, and then she said, "Have you spoken with Rebecca lately?"

"Yes, of course. Last night. She sounded good," Jack said.

"What did she say?"

"The usual. Overloaded with work but she's doing well. She loves seeing you."

"Anything else?" Sadie said, pushing on.

After a brief silence, Jack said, "Is there something you want to tell me?"

Sadie made her tone nonchalant. "Not really. She didn't say anything to you about a boy?"

"No. What boy?"

She said Kurt's name with a flourish.

"Kurt who?"

Sadie heard Jack tap impatiently on his desk with a pen or a pencil, and she knew she had him hooked. "Kurt Lichter. He's German and wears a black leather motorcycle jacket."

"German. A leather motorcycle jacket?"

"And high black leather boots and a big cross earring dangles from his ear."

The tapping got louder, like a distress signal in Morse code. "For God's sake, Mother, what about him?"

"She's dating him. What's all that noise? Sounds like you have a woodpecker there with you?" Sadie said. The tapping stopped.

"You mean dating seriously? Where did she meet him?" he said, his voice tense.

"I'm not sure. Who knows?" she said, looking out the window.

"She never mentioned seeing anyone to me."

"Listen, Jack, don't worry and don't say anything. Let Rebecca tell you about it herself."

"I was coming to New York in a couple of months anyway. I'll make it sooner."

Sadie looked out of the window and watched the sun disappear behind a cloud, pleased with herself for accomplishing her mission. She said goodbye to her son and hung up the phone.

The doorbell rang. She headed out of the kitchen to the front door and looked through the peephole and was surprised to see Rabbi Feldman. She opened the door. "Rabbi . . . I wasn't expecting you."

"I was across the street. What, I can't drop in on an old friend?"

Rabbi Feldman took her arm as they walked through the foyer. "You heard about what happened to our synagogue?" he said.

"Yes, yes. What an awful thing. I wanted to come to see you, but I was too afraid of what I might find."

When they reached the living room, the rabbi helped Sadie into her chair. "Sit down and let me make you a cup of tea. I have a very big favor to ask of you," he said, sitting on the couch across from her.

"You know the beautiful mural that we both love inside our synagogue?" the rabbi said leaning forward.

"Yes, of course. Max, may he rest in peace, and I admired it from the minute we first stepped foot in your synagogue. It reminded Max of a temple in Warsaw he and his family attended before the war. He was Bar Mitzvahed there."

"I was wondering if you could lend a hand in its restoration."

"Me . . . you're asking me?" she said.

"Yes, I am asking you. I want you to supervise, be like an art director."

"Oh, Rabbi, I don't know . . . it was another lifetime ago. I'm not so sure I could resurrect that part of me."

"I'm just asking you to think about it while I make the tea," he said as he rose and made his way toward the kitchen.

Would she dare? Was she up to the task? These questions burned inside her brain as she leaned back in her chair. Just the thought of it made her hands tremble.

Chapter 24

Kurt darted through the corridors of New York University Medical Center, quickly scanning the faces of everyone he encountered. He had called Rebecca after his confrontation with Sadie, desperate to see her. He raced around a corner and spotted her, flanked by other students wearing white lab coats.

He sprinted toward her. "Rebecca, Rebecca."

She ushered him into a discreet corner. "I only have a few minutes between classes. What's wrong?"

Kurt spoke softly. "Your grandmother knew about our having coffee together and she even accused me of manipulating you. She was very angry with me. I tried to apologize to her for our last meeting, but she didn't even acknowledge it."

"I'm sorry. She nearly bit my head off as well. I just thought it would help if I put in a good word for you. I'm so sorry it backfired. I told you it would take time. She's very stubborn."

"That's okay, you tried. And she also thought that you and I . . ."

Rebecca blushed. "I know, I know. That generation. They don't understand that a woman and a man can be just friends."

"Yes. Very old school. I don't want to take up any more of your time. Thank you, Rebecca, for trying."

"Oh, that's okay. I'd better get going."

Rebecca started to leave but then said, "I don't ordinarily do this . . . but do you want to get together sometime? Maybe for coffee or a movie or something?"

Kurt, hesitantly, "But what about your Grandmother?"

"I can keep a secret if you can."

"Yes, I would like that, but if it's a movie—anything but a Scorsese film."

Rebecca looked at him questioningly.

"Never mind, it's a long story," he said, amused at his own joke. It pleased him that he could make a joke about Karin now that she had become part of his past. He wondered if maybe Rebecca was his future. With his luck, who knows?

The next morning, only flickers of light shone through the stained glass windows of the synagogue casting a strange, almost eerie glow onto Kurt's face, as he stood on his ladder working on Moses leading the Hebrews out of Egypt. His concentration was intermittently broken by thoughts of seeing Rebecca again, but Moses and his flock kept summoning him back to the task at hand: finishing that section.

For the past week, he'd been immersed in the desert surrounded by scores of Hebrews, wearing dark robes of blue, red and green, treading through the desert sands. He felt as if he was part of this mass departure—hot, sweaty and hungry, guided by their leader Moses, with his long gray beard, holding a long staff, wearing a dark brown robe with a white head covering.

He now focused on the sky above the wanderers, using broad

brush strokes for the muted blue-gray sky with white clouds, a hint of yellow shining through. It contrasted beautifully with the mixed grains of yellow, brown and beige sand that he had created with smaller brush strokes the day before. Kurt made sure he used the original colors as he remembered them, but also added additional colors when needed. But, most importantly, all of the vandals' blasphemous symbols and words of hatred had been purged from that section.

He heard Rabbi Feldman clear his throat. "Kurt," the rabbi said and strained his neck up to see the recreated pale blue sky streaked with colossal illuminated milk-white clouds. "Oh, I love what you did to the sky and the sands . . . I think it's even more striking than before."

"Thank you, Rabbi," Kurt said, relieved.

"Actually, the mural was in desperate need of a facelift, and you've done a marvelous job with this section. I feel like I'm one of the thousands of Hebrews centuries ago, migrating through the treacherous desert."

At least the rabbi was pleased, although he was the only one who had seen it so far. Kurt was struck with how similar he and the rabbi were affected by it.

The sound of knocking interrupted them. They both turned their heads to the back.

"I'll get it . . . I'll get it," the rabbi said as he headed toward the lobby.

Sadie, her good arm linked through Rebecca's, stared blankly at the synagogue's newly stained front door and was thankful the exterior had been restored to its original state before the defacement. She was terrified to view the desecration on the other side, anticipating that it might thrust her back to 1938, when she had witnessed *Kristallnacht*.

She had only been a child but clearly remembered the sounds of glass shattering, the screams of panic and outrage, and the next day, the shards of glass that lined the streets reflecting the gray November light. Red paint and swastikas maligned the façades of all the Jewish owned stores and buildings on her street.

She had to summon her strength. Rabbi Feldman was eager for her to play a major role in the synagogue's restoration, and she couldn't disappoint him.

"Sadie, I'm so glad you decided to come," the rabbi said as he opened the door.

Sadie nodded solemnly, beset with apprehension.

He turned to Rebecca and smiled. "And you must be Rebecca—Sadie has sung your praises so many times, it's like a full fledge opera," he said, taking Rebecca's hand. "And thank you for bringing your grandmother."

"You're welcome, Rabbi Feldman, but I'm not sure why we're here," Rebecca said, glancing over at Sadie. "She's been so secretive . . . so mysterious."

"What? An old woman can't be tight-lipped once in awhile? I have to tell everybody everything?"

"Okay, Sadie, it's okay . . . let's go inside," the rabbi said, gently taking Sadie's arm and ushering her through the lobby. The walls were once again white, but Sadie noticed the tile floor still had remnants of red paint embedded in the grout. She felt like maybe this wasn't such a good idea.

As they walked inside the interior, Sadie surveyed each section of the mural until she came upon a large red streaked swastika still painted over Moses receiving the Ten Commandments.

Remembering the last time she saw one that close up, her stomach tightened and her body began to tremble. Every morning in the camp at roll call she witnessed a sea of swastikas on armbands raised high as the camp guards saluted their fuehrer with a resounding *"Seig Heil,"* not knowing if she was going to be singled out and shot or beaten for something they said you did, whether she was guilty or not.

"Grandma, are you okay?"

She could hear Rebecca's voice, the rising panic in her tone, but couldn't respond.

When Sadie reached the part of the mural where Moses leads the Hebrews out of Egypt, she caught Kurt's eye and was struck. A vision of Kurt in an S.S. uniform, as he'd been in her recent nightmares, flashed in her brain.

"Grandma?"

Sadie blinked several times to obliterate that image, but it was difficult to erase. She didn't understand why this insolent German boy was here, working in a synagogue, repairing their beautiful mural. It was nothing short of sacrilegious.

She could hear Rebecca reproaching Rabbi Feldman and felt it was wrong of her to do so, but didn't have the breath to stop her.

"Rabbi, maybe this is too much for her. I don't think she should she be here," Rebecca was saying.

"It's okay, Rebecca," the rabbi said and took Sadie's arm and steered her toward a seat. "Sadie, come, come and sit down."

Sadie wrestled herself back to the present. She allowed the rabbi to guide her to a seat close to where Kurt was painting. Rebecca sat next to her, and she noticed her granddaughter glancing up at Kurt. Sadie wondered what was really going on between those two. Was her fear of Kurt and Rebecca seeing each other really justified? Oh my God, this couldn't be happening.

"Sadie, look at what Kurt has done so far. He has been working diligently every day and making excellent progress," the rabbi said, pointing to where Kurt was working.

Sadie slowly stood up and gazed at Moses leading the Hebrews out of Egypt. "The colors are too bright—I should have my sunglasses on. It looks like it's in 3D, like those god-awful movies they make now," she said squinting. "*Oy vey*, where's my beautiful, delicately hued Moses with his flock trekking through the crumbling desert?" she said, and turned toward the rabbi. "It was much more beautiful the old way—the way it was when we . . . my Max, may he rest in peace, and I first saw it. Why did you hire this *shegetz* to repair our mural? He's determined to ruin it, to make us regret our history."

She stared up at Kurt defiantly and noticed the anger in his face. He looked like he was about to explode, but then he peeked over at Rebecca and remained silent.

"Grandma, how could you yell at Kurt like that? It's obvious how hard he's been working. And considering what he has to work with, I think he's doing a great job," Rebecca said, visibly shaken.

Sadie felt simultaneously justified and ashamed at her outburst. It had been a long time since she let go like that. But when she saw how Rebecca was affected by it, she wished she had handled it differently—less harshly.

Rabbi Feldman gently eased Sadie back in her seat. "Please, please calm down, Sadela. We have Kurt restoring our synagogue because he comes at a good price, zero dollars. He's a volunteer, Sadela," he said softly. "When you first saw the mural it was already decades old. I think he's doing a good job adding new life to it, and with your guidance he will do even better," the rabbi said and pointed to the severely damaged section of the mural that hadn't been touched yet.

"See, Sadie over there . . . that's the part I was telling you about."

"Yes, yes . . . Hmmm. It was once Moses on Mt. Sinai receiving the Ten Commandments," Sadie said.

"Now, it's one big red disaster," Rabbi Feldman said.

"Could someone please tell me what is going on here?" Rebecca asked.

"Your grandmother is going to help Kurt restore our mural."

"Help? How?"

"Actually, she's going to supervise him," the rabbi said.

"I said I'd think about it . . . take a look. That's all," Sadie said, still staring at the mural.

"Rebecca, your grandmother used to be an artist."

"Oh my God, I never knew that. When?"

"A million lifetimes ago," Sadie whispered.

Kurt climbed down from the ladder, stepped forward and had the audacity to stand next to Rebecca, their shoulders almost touching.

"I . . . I can hardly remember what it looked like before, Mrs. Seidenberg. I only saw it that once when I brought you and Mrs. Feingold here for . . . *Shabbos*."

Sadie was shocked that Kurt remembered the right word and from the look on his face, he was, too.

Her eyes fixed on the rabbi. How could she refuse him? It was he who helped her readjust to life after her hellish years in Auschwitz. He was so young then, fresh out rabbinical school, and had helped her and Max so much through group sessions with other survivors and individual counseling sessions to deal with her continuous nightmares and paranoia. Always looking over her shoulder, afraid she'd be abducted and sent back to her tortured existence in the camp. And, after all she and Max went through to get to America, almost a year being stuck in the refugee camp, even marrying there so that they could stay together. Finally, the U.N. workers there were able to locate her Aunt Sylvia in New York, who sponsored both of them to emigrate to America. When they passed the Statue of Liberty, she squeezed Max's hand so tightly, he gasped from the pain.

And when they arrived in New York, she and Max felt like pariahs as American Jews were afraid to even talk to these walking skeletons with their left arms blighted with six black numbers, and treated them as if they were somehow responsible for their own brutalization. She could see it in their eyes, the mixture of contempt, fear and pity.

After Max died, Sadie didn't know if she'd ever get over her grief. How would she be able to go on without him? He was her crutch, her rock. Rabbi Feldman with his infinite compassion was there to help her cope. With mixed emotions, she made her decision.

"So, I will help this little *pisher* . . . or else, we could end up with a blond blue-eyed Moses up in the Alps somewhere."

Chapter 25

The setting sun cast a pink glow in the hazy sky over the muddy East River with bits of debris floating on top. Kurt and Rebecca strolled along the Promenade among other couples holding hands, leisurely walking and joggers on their nightly run.

Kurt casually took her hand, not wanting to be too forward. Once her hand was firmly in his, he was able to relax. His fear that she was just interested in him as a friend was calmed. He felt relaxed and was able to spend their first time alone together opening himself up to her. Talking about their backgrounds, sharing the similarities and stark differences, he was struck at how different their upbringings were. She was much like Karin, a child of privilege, their dreams of realizing their goals within reach. And apparently their taste in men was also alike. Both were attracted to boys that didn't come with an automatic stamp of approval from their demanding parents.

Although Rebecca radiated warmth and sweetness, he also detected a hint of a rebellious spirit reminiscent of his ex.

"So you're also an only child," Kurt said.

"Yes, my mother couldn't have any more children after me," Rebecca said.

Kurt posed another question, before she had a chance to ask him about why his mother never had another child. The truth was that she couldn't handle another child after him. Perhaps because he was too much for her or once she had him she realized she lacked the nurturing component of motherhood. There was no way of spinning that into something flattering to him or his mother.

"It must have been very difficult, losing your mother at sixteen," he said softly, squeezing her hand.

"Yes, it was . . . I still miss her so much. She was gentle, caring and supportive, the exact opposite of my dad. She was also a lawyer but worked for the city as a public defender. Always helping people less fortunate than her. I never could figure out how the two of them got together. I guess it was a yin yang thing. But, in the last year before she died she was in so much pain, it was very hard on all of us. It's the reason I'm in med school—to be an oncologist specializing in ovarian cancer. I was thinking of going into cancer research, but working with women with cancer seems more appealing to me. My mother's doctor, the top oncologist in Los Angeles, a real hotshot and a friend of my father, wasn't as compassionate as he could have been."

He waited a moment before asking another question, digesting what she just told him. If anyone possessed the necessary qualities of an empathetic cancer doctor, it would be Rebecca.

"And your father . . . what's he like?" he said.

"A complete control freak. He's one of those people who's so bottled up, if you loosen the cap, even a little, you're afraid of what will come gushing out."

"My father is like that, too. But he doesn't keep anything inside. When he loses his temper, you know exactly what will come out, his fists, even now that I'm grown. My mother just sits there watching the both of us like she's at a boxing match. In the end, she always backs him up."

"Oh, I'm sorry to hear that . . . and what about your grandparents? Are they still alive?"

"My maternal grandfather died when I was twelve and my maternal grandmother died last year. They lived in Munich, I hardly ever saw them. My paternal grandmother died when I was a baby, and my paternal grandfather moved in with us . . . a very broken old man. He hardly ever speaks."

He saw hesitancy in her face. She waited a moment.

"I'm almost afraid to ask, but I know it's something my grandmother would want to know, what did your grandfather do during the war?"

Kurt knew that it was a strong possibility she'd ask this question. Why wouldn't she want to know if he was an S.S. officer or a camp guard or just a soldier fighting the war in Europe? He would if the situation was in reverse, he'd sure as hell would want to know if a member of her family participated in the Final Solution.

"He never spoke one word about it. When I was a boy in grammar school we studied World War Two. I came home one day and asked him: Grandpa, were you a soldier in the war? What did you do there? I was so curious."

Kurt looked squarely at Rebecca. "He just glared at me, his eyes glazed over as if he was in unbearable pain. He frightened me so much and then he told me that such things must never be spoken about. You can never ask me about the war again and I never did."

"My grandmother never talks to me about the war either or her family, or her life before or after Auschwitz. I guess it is just too horrible to talk about."

Instinctively, he put his arm around her and led her to the railing. He looked out into night and saw the moon reflected in the rippling dirty river. He noticed she was also looking at the moon. Its light illuminated the red highlights in her hair.

Kurt turned to Rebecca, gazed into her eyes, impulsively wrapped her in his arms, and kissed her.

Chapter 26

Sadie sat in an aisle seat in the synagogue. Kurt, a few seats away facing her, had an open sketchpad in his lap and a charcoal pencil in his hand. He was ready.

"So, what do you know about Moses?" Sadie asked, testing him.

"Moses? A little. Why?"

"You're restoring a synagogue. You're painting Moses—you should know who he was, for God's sake."

He conjured up a memory of his early Sunday school days. "He was a prophet and the leader of the Jewish people," he said, responding as if he was still in grade school.

"Okay, you get a D plus. What else?"

"He led the Israelites out of Egypt and into Israel. David gave me some literature about Judaism."

"The story of Moses, of Exodus, is a story of escaping incredible pain and suffering to a better life. You are probably too young to know about that. To know what it's like to be trapped in a terrible situation."

"No, I am not too young," Kurt said. "I know exactly what you mean."

She was surprised by this *nudnik's* quick and confident response, but didn't believe a word of it. What would he know about such things? She pointed to the section of the mural where baby Moses in a basket of bulrushes was discovered by the Pharaoh's daughter.

"You see it started with the Pharaoh's order that every son born of an Israelite should be thrown into the river to drown," Sadie said, gesturing to that section. "But, Moses's mother put her baby son in a basket of bulrushes and set it afloat in the Nile River. The Pharaoh's daughter found the baby, felt sorry for him and took him out of the water. She named him Moses, which in Hebrew means to draw out."

"And then he grew up to be the leader of the Jews?"

"Actually, it wasn't until many years later, when Moses had grown up that he visited the Israelites, his people. He witnessed an Egyptian beating a Hebrew slave, lost his temper, killed the Egyptian and buried him in the sand. The Pharaoh heard of the murder and ordered his soldiers to kill Moses . . ."

"Moses killed someone?"

"Yes, and escaped to the land of Midian. He lived among the Midians and later married Zipporah, the daughter of their priest, a *shiksa*," she said, knowing full well he wouldn't know what the word meant.

"A *shiksa*?"

"A girl who isn't Jewish. Anyway, to make a long story short, one day when Moses was tending sheep in the wilderness near Sinai, a bush suddenly caught fire."

Sadie pointed to the section of the mural where Moses stood before the burning bush. Kurt turned his head toward that section.

"God called to Moses from the bush and told him that he was sending him back to Egypt to lead his people, the Israelites, out of slavery."

"Why Moses?" Kurt asked. Sadie was surprised by the look on Kurt's face. He was totally engrossed in the story. She'd thought he'd be bored to death by now.

"That's exactly what Moses asked. Why me? Who am I that anyone would listen to me? You know Moses had a speech impediment and was not a very good speaker. But God chose him anyway."

Sadie looked over to the section where Moses led the Israelites through the parted sea. "He gave Moses the power to part the Red Sea so that he could lead the Israelites out of Egypt. God passed his laws on Mt. Sinai onto him for the Israelites to obey. Moses carved two tablets out of stone and wrote the Ten Commandments on them."

Sadie and Kurt surveyed what remained of that section of the mural. Only part of Moses' head was visible: his long white hair. The rest of Moses' face and body was hidden under a splatter of red paint. Kurt began to sketch. "Was Moses a very old man then?"

"He wasn't young."

Sadie remained silent while Kurt sketched. After a while, Sadie said, "Let me see what you have there."

Kurt shielded his work with his hands. "Not yet. I just started."

"I only want to see what you have so far."

His face flushed, he lifted up the pad and held it close to his chest. "No, no, not yet. It's not very good. I'm very rusty."

As much as she fought to maintain her original attitude toward this little *pisher*, Sadie understood how Kurt felt—to be an artist who hasn't created art for a long time. She could no longer remember what it felt like to have a piece of charcoal in her hands.

The sun was setting on the Lower East Side as Kurt entered the Jewish Seniors Outreach Center. He found David typing on his computer.

"David, would you mind if I used one of your computers? I need to do some research for my work at the synagogue."

"Sure. Use the one over there." David pointed to the desk to the right of him. "You're working miracles, according to Rabbi Feldman."

"He said that?"

"He really admires your work and dedication. He said you're doing a superb job. I was very glad to hear that. I wasn't so sure you'd work out so well."

Kurt beamed. He was even shocked himself at how committed he was to completing this project and how he was able to access all of his past art training and knowledge into his painting. Instead of dreading each day he had to work on the mural, he was energized by it, and to be praised so highly for it was mind-boggling.

He took a seat at the desk allocated to him, powered up the computer and googled *Moses—pictures*. Eighteen million, five hundred thousand results popped up. Kurt clicked on the first choice, Images for Moses, which displayed Moses in various scenarios from the Bible. He selected one picture after another: Michelangelo's bust of Moses depicted Moses with a very stern expression on his face; an ennobled, proud Charlton Heston as Moses clutching the two stone tablets with the Ten Commandments carved on them; a young, angry Moses holding the two smashed tablets; and an older, white haired Moses on Mt. Sinai. He studied each one and closed his eyes for a moment.

He picked up his sketchpad and turned to the page that had the beginning drawing of Moses he started at the synagogue. He grabbed his charcoal pencil and feverishly began to draw an elderly, fiery Moses.

Chapter 27

"This is so delicious. You're a very good cook," Kurt said, taking a big bite out of a piece of barbecued chicken. He sat across from Rebecca at her small round café-style glass-top table adorned with a lighted candle and a bottle of Merlot. He was thrilled to be in her compact, cleverly designed studio East Side apartment near her Medical School.

"Well, I didn't exactly cook it myself. I picked it up at a barbeque place around the corner," she said with a grin.

"Maybe some time I can make dinner for you. I make a good Wiener schnitzel."

"I don't think I ever had Wiener schnitzel."

A phone rang and Rebecca reached down in her jeans pocket and pulled out her cell and answered it. "Hello? Oh, Daddy, hi." After listening for a minute, her expression changed from happy to curious to concerned. "Okay, I'll see you then. I'd better get back to my books. Bye now."

Rebecca clicked off the phone, put it back in her pocket and drained her glass of wine.

"My father is coming here in a couple of weeks. I thought he would be visiting next month. But he said he had to change his plans to be here earlier. He didn't say why, and he sounded strange."

"Strange how?"

"As if he was keeping something from me."

"Maybe he has a surprise for you. He probably just misses you. I know I would."

"Yeah, he misses me. He also likes to keep a close eye on me," she said and poured herself another glass of wine and gulped down half of it. "And my father's surprises aren't generally happy ones."

"What would he have to worry about? You do all the right things," Kurt said.

"That's me, all right. Rebecca Seidenberg, world's most perfect daughter . . . so he thinks."

"I'm Kurt Lichter, world's worst son." He extended his hand to her. "Pleased to meet you."

Rebecca shook his hand and laughed.

"We make a good pair, don't you think?" he said, pausing for a moment. "Do you think your father would like me?"

Rebecca took another gulp of wine. "You know how fathers are. No one is good enough for their little girl."

Kurt studied her thoughtfully. "Would he not like me because of the way I look . . . my earring and everything?"

"He might be a bit concerned. I'm only just starting to get used to it myself," she said, smirking, and snatched up the dirty dishes. "Really, you shouldn't worry about that. The most important thing right now is who is going to wash and who's going to dry."

Kurt laughed and followed Rebecca over to the sink in the small kitchen alcove behind the dining area. She tossed him a dish towel, then began scrubbing and rinsing the dinner dishes and handing them to him to dry.

Kurt performed his delegated task with only one thought in mind: Would he and Rebecca make love tonight? He had been wondering how it would feel to hold her in his arms, caress her beautiful, naked body. He was possessed with these thoughts every night before falling asleep. And yet Karin was the first and only girl he had sex with when he was sixteen, except for a one night fling with one of his high school classmates when Karin was away with her parents, Christmas, senior year.

He wondered how sex with Rebecca would be. He had a feeling that she'd be more experienced than he. For one thing, she was a year older. A lot can happen in one year and the way she looked at him, her simmering eyes emitting a desire that was impossible to misinterpret. It made him feel that it would be different with her than with his mentor, Karin, who was pretty much in control. She taught him the moves, the speed and how to assure mutual orgasms almost every time. With her, sex always felt like he was satisfying her insatiable hunger that was more physical than emotional. And with Brigitte, his one night fling, he was very awkward, hesitant, flopping up and down like a fish on dry land.

After the dishes were washed and dried, Kurt seized the moment. To wait even another minute would have been torture. He took Rebecca in his arms and kissed her. He felt her soft, sweet mouth press against his. The kiss was both heated and tender. He could tell from the intensity of her kiss that the feeling was mutual. They hastily undressed each other and Rebecca led Kurt over to her bed, which was in its own alcove, a dimly lit, secluded spot.

Rebecca slid onto her bed and Kurt gently moved on top of her. They gazed into each other eyes. He placed soft, baby kisses on her forehead and cheeks. They moved slowly together in perfect harmony with their eyes fixed on each other. Karin always closed her eyes during sex; he would look at her but she never looked back at him.

This was such a different experience—being able to share the joy, the pleasure that was openly reflected in their faces.

Chapter 28

Kurt held onto Sadie's arm as they approached the synagogue. She glanced at a rolled-up piece of drawing paper under his arm.

"So is this your Moses?" she said.

He nodded and opened the door with a key that Rabbi Feldman had entrusted to him and switched on the light. The lobby sparkled with a newly scrubbed tile floor, all of the red drippings erased.

He ushered Sadie inside. Sunlight splashed through the stained glass windows and bathed the interior with speckles of multicolored rays of light. He switched on the back wall light, guided Sadie to the front row, assisted her into the aisle seat, and hovered.

She gazed up at him. "Are you going to show me your sketch, or what?"

"I'm not sure it's quite right yet."

"What am I, the *New York Times* art critic? I'm just an old lady. Let me see it, for God's sake."

Kurt hesitantly unrolled the drawing, grabbed both ends, and revealed it to her. He scrutinized Sadie's face anxiously as she studied the drawing. What was she thinking? He never liked listening to criticism. He never got used to it.

"I don't know what you were afraid of. It is a good start. I have to say you're kinda talented."

"You'd be the only one who thinks so."

"What is it with you? All of a sudden you're Mr. Humble?"

Kurt rolled up his drawing and sat down next to her. "I was studying Fine Arts at the Arts University of Berlin. The first year I concentrated on realism: portraits, still lifes and landscapes. By the second year I became very influenced by the Surrealists: Dali, Kahlo, Ernst. My paintings also reflected my politics—how I felt about the decaying, violent world around me. My teachers hated my work. They said my work was too eccentric, too political. Surrealistic painting was obsolete now. They were always on my back and eventually I was forced out."

"I find that hard to believe. They threw you out because you didn't paint the way they wanted you to?" Sadie said.

"Well, yes, and I lost my temper once or twice."

"That I believe. What happened?"

He lowered his voice. "I got so mad at my Fine Arts professor, Mr. Aschenbrenner, it was after weeks of him berating me about my paintings in front of the other students. I don't remember exactly what happened. I started swinging and punched him a few times. My mother begged him not to press charges. Instead, they kicked me out. It was a great embarrassment to my family. They have never forgiven me for it."

"You couldn't study somewhere else?"

"Not in Germany. Anyway, that was the most prestigious place to study art, and my joy of creating faded away. Even though the professor never pressed charges, the incident remained on my school record. As a favor to my parents, it was sealed."

*   *   *

Sadie stared at Kurt for a long moment. "I would have given anything to go to art school. Anything . . ."

She stopped abruptly. She couldn't bear talking about those years, particularly to a young German. It wouldn't be right.

"Why didn't you?"

Sadie shook herself out of her past.

"That's not important now. We don't have all day to talk. Let me see your sketch again."

Kurt unrolled his drawing and showed it to Sadie.

"I like your Moses. But his face is too angry, too ferocious. Moses loved, respected and obeyed God, but he was also very afraid. There he was, forty days and forty nights with God. He never wanted to be the leader of his people. He never felt he had the right. We need to see all that in his face."

She gazed at the sketch once again. She couldn't really express in words what she meant. There was only one way to communicate to Kurt how to improve his Moses. Her face swelled with emotion. Does she dare? Would she still know how? Sadie had a sudden impulse to draw—to show him, not just tell him what she was talking about. How long has it been? Too many years ago. She carefully removed the sling from her arm.

"Hand me a piece of charcoal, please."

"Your arm? Is that okay?"

"It's fine. The doctor said I can take the sling off and use my arm once in awhile. It won't hurt the healing process."

Kurt leaned over his paint box on a seat behind him and removed a piece of charcoal and handed it to Sadie. She rolled it back and forth, getting the feel of it in her hand. Her eyes welled up with tears.

"For me too it has been a long, long time. Do you . . . would you mind if I add something to your sketch? I'm not sure I even remember how."

"No, no. Of course not. Go ahead," Kurt said.

Sadie added a few lines to Moses's face, at first cautiously but after a few minutes, the charcoal seemed to move about on its own, changing the facial expression quite drastically. It was now a fearful, reverential Moses. She couldn't believe how easy it was for her after all this time. She felt as if she was being guided by divine intervention, as if she was meant to have a piece of charcoal in her hand again. It was time.

After Sadie finished shading some of the lines with her fingers, she gave the drawing to Kurt. He examined it for several minutes. "Mrs. Seidenberg, this is remarkable. With a few lines and shading, you really changed his expression. I don't know if I can do that."

"Yes, yes you can. Don't worry, I know you can. Go, go get the ladder."

Kurt placed the drawing on the seat next to Sadie, hurried over to Moses parting the waters section of the mural and grabbed the ladder. He moved it over to Moses receiving the Ten Commandments on Mt. Sinai, then snatched up the sketch, rushed up the ladder and taped it onto the wall.

Sadie watched attentively as Kurt lifted up his brush and began to paint, reviving the bloodied Moses, glancing back and forth from her sketch to the mural, transforming Moses into a more terrified, agonized prophet.

Kurt waited outside the entrance of the NYU Medical School Library, watching the many people exiting the building.

He spotted Rebecca winding her way through the revolving door with a large rucksack on her back which got stuck half-way through. Kurt smiled as he watched her twist and turn her body to free herself.

He rushed toward her, shouting her name, weaving his way through the crowd of people in between.

Rebecca leaned forward and kissed him, nearly toppling over from the weight on her back. Kurt caught her and they both stumbled to maintain their balance.

"What do you have in your rucksack, concrete?" He stepped behind her. "Here, let me help you." Kurt lifted her pack off her back and hoisted it onto his own.

He led her away from the library and toward a corner coffee shop at the end of the block.

"I wasn't sure you'd make it with all the work you have to do to finish up at the synagogue," Rebecca said.

"I wanted to see you even if it was only for a minute."

"I'm afraid a minute is all you're going to get. I have to spend some serious time with cranial and spinal nerves tonight. I have an exam tomorrow."

"Just don't get too serious," he said teasingly.

"I'll try, but you know how nerves are. They're very sensual," she said in a low, seductive voice.

Kurt stopped and looked at her only to realize she was teasing him again. He liked this about her, that in spite of her very serious studies, she enjoyed life.

They entered The Cozy Corner Coffee Shop and had no trouble finding a booth. They slid in across from each other. Kurt unloaded the rucksack and set it down next to him. They both picked up their menus.

A twenty-something waitress with tattoo sleeves on both arms, her curly fire-engine red hair secured in a hairnet, appeared from behind the counter and took their orders: two coffees and two slices of New York cheesecake. Kurt checked out her arms, which resembled

15th century religious frescos and suddenly felt as if he could have added more white and yellow to his Moses receiving the Ten Commandments.

"Is the mural almost finished?" Rebecca asked. "Grandma told me it has to be done by Friday sundown and it's already Tuesday. Are you nervous?"

"It will be done by *shabbos*, opening night, and yes, I'm very anxious. Nobody has seen it other than your grandmother and the rabbi."

"So it's 'by *shabbos*' now. You're becoming an honorary Jew, whether you like it or not." She paused for a moment. "How is it going with her now? Has it been any easier? She hasn't talked about it much."

"You should see how she improved my sketch of Moses. She's an amazing artist."

He didn't want to say the truth—which was that he was always treading on thin ice with Sadie. He never knew exactly what would set her off. He had to think before he said anything to her—an entirely new experience for him. And it was the same with Rebecca. She was a pit bull when it came to Sadie and would bite his head off at a moment's notice if he did anything that would upset her grandmother. But was he really becoming an honorary Jew? Three months ago, he couldn't imagine it. But now, he spent every day and night in the company of Jews, learning their customs, language and witnessing firsthand their remarkable resilience. One day their beautiful old synagogue was almost ruined beyond recognition, and the next day Rabbi Feldman and his flock were on the job of renewal.

"It's shocking," Rebecca said, leaning forward. "I never knew anything about her ever being an artist nor did my father—he was as surprised as I was."

"I asked about her art background, but it seemed too painful for her to talk about," Kurt said, taking the silverware out of the rolled up paper napkin.

He understood Sadie's silence. His grandfather had never spoken a word about his past or his family or anything else for that matter before or after the war. Although one was a Jew, a victim, and the other a German, an aggressor, they both were uncommunicative when it came to the Holocaust.

"Will he be there Friday night?"

"Who?"

"Your father?" he said, wondering why she was stalling.

"Oh, no, he'll still be in D.C."

The waitress delivered their orders, and Rebecca dove into her cheesecake immediately.

"Let's not talk about my father. It's enough I have to call him every night to assure him I'm still alive. Let's talk about this cheesecake. Is this yummy or what?"

"Maybe I can meet him when he comes in?" Kurt said, gulping down his coffee as if it were a stiff drink.

"Oh . . . maybe," she said and scoffed down the last of her cheesecake.

He could tell from her response, that for some reason, she was very uneasy about him meeting her father. She'd said that he was very critical of anyone wanting to date his daughter, and Kurt understood that. Karin's father wanted her to date only boys from wealthy families and never approved of him, a son of a postman, but that never stood in the way of their relationship. Somehow, with Rebecca, this seemed more serious than a matter of money, and he decided that it was better for him not to demand an answer and to remain silent. No sense starting trouble now. He had enough on his plate for the time being.

Rebecca stood and grabbed her rucksack. "I'd better go and tackle these books."

They slid out of their seats. Kurt carefully placed her rucksack on her back and they headed out of the shop.

"I'll see you Friday night," he said, planting a tender, brief kiss on her lips.

"The restored synagogue's premiere," Rebecca said.

"Yes, and I feel like I will be standing in a crowded auditorium, naked and surrounded by blank walls like in a dream that suddenly turns into a nightmare."

"That I'd like to see!"

She laughed and threw her arms around him. He held her tightly, and they kissed again, longer, more passionately. He was relieved that the strain between them had passed.

Chapter 29

Kurt stepped out of the synagogue for a breath of air. It was early evening and the sun was inching its way below the horizon. Soon it would disappear, night would fall and the Sabbath would begin. He noticed a police car parked across the street and was glad it was there for the debut of the newly renovated synagogue. It couldn't hurt to have extra security.

He went back inside and cleared away his paint box and rags from the floor in front of Moses receiving the Ten Commandments, walked toward the rabbi's office to the right of the podium, but stopped first, taking a few steps back to view the entire mural section by section. The faded, crumbled paint was now replaced with fresh, vibrant colors. All of the desecration was erased.

Moses aged accordingly, his brown hair streaking gray, then dazzling white. His face developed more pronounced wrinkles and deep cavernous lines from segment to segment.

Kurt smiled with a sense of satisfaction and pride at what he had accomplished with Sadie's guidance, knowing that he couldn't have done it without her. He watched Rabbi Feldman as he made a few last minute corrections to his opening night *Shabbos* sermon. He had grown quite fond of this man and was starting to feel that he was kind of the grandfather he never had.

Rabbi Feldman must have sensed Kurt's presence and popped his head up. "The mural is perfect, Kurt, even better than before. Moses really looks like he actually has been wandering the desert for forty days and forty nights. A real accomplishment."

"Thank you, Rabbi. I owe it all to Sadie's incredible direction and I hope your congregation will like it as much as you do."

"Don't worry, they will."

He glanced down at his notebook. "I just hope my sermon will address the wide range of emotions I know will be present tonight—the young with their hot tempers and a thirst for revenge. Last week, I spent hours talking to the young men who had helped paint the lobby into abandoning their search all over lower Manhattan for the culprits responsible for the vandalism and to leave that job to the police. For the older members, it is a different story. The Nazi symbols and hate speech revive their horrendous memories of the Holocaust, whether they lived through it firsthand or through the documentaries and news footage of piles of bones found all over Eastern Europe after the war ended."

They were interrupted by Ben Levine, the volunteer security guard, ushering a TV crew inside. He had them set up their cameras to the right of the double doors.

"Rabbi, who are they?"

"Oh yes, I forgot to mention that. They're from New York One, a local cable TV news channel. They're covering the synagogue's restoration. They've already filmed the exterior and lobby and now they will film the interior of the synagogue, the mural and my sermon. I think it is going to be a feature story. I'm not exactly sure what or when or if they'll actually air the piece, but any coverage will be good

for us. We were already able to cover the costs of the repairs from con-
tributions that came in from all over New York City. People always
love a comeback story."

What the fuck! If he didn't already feel pressured before, Kurt
certainly did now. How many people will actually see his work? His
head began ache. Shit! That was all he needed now—one of his tension headaches.

He continued to the back office, dropped off the rags and his
paint box and changed into a black suit, white shirt and gray tie that
Tony had lent him for the occasion. He wanted to look like a gentleman on opening night. The pants were a bit short, but not enough to
notice, or so he hoped. He removed a pair of black leather dress shoes,
also Tony's, from a brown paper shopping bag, sat down in the rabbi's
desk chair and put them on. He had to manipulate the laces so that his
feet would fit into them as they were too narrow for his feet. He then
reached in the pocket of his jeans that he had laid on the back of the
chair, pulled out his comb, slicked his hair back behind his ears, and
removed his earring. When he stood up, he instantly knew that his
feet would be giving him trouble for the rest of the evening.

He picked up the yarmulke the rabbi had left for him on the desk
and placed it on top of his head, centered. He no longer believed that
as a German it was improper or inappropriate to wear a yarmulke as he
had his first time in the synagogue. He had spent the last several weeks
there with Rabbi Feldman and Sadie, forging the most positive rela-
tionships he had ever experienced with older adults. Now, he somehow felt that wearing a suit, tie and yarmulke was a true expression
of his fondness and respect for them. He never imagined this would
happen. He was positive that if he hadn't been forced to repair the
synagogue, renewing his commitment to art and bonding with Sadie
through their shared passion, he would have been shipped back to

Berlin by now. And, of course, his relationship with Rebecca gave him an added incentive to remain in New York.

Upon entering his office, Rabbi Feldman complimented Kurt on how dapper he looked. He opened up a door to a small closet, retrieved his suit jacket, and put it on.

"Well, the time has come to inaugurate our restored synagogue. I'm going to spruce up a bit. We should both look debonair."

He pulled out the top drawer of his desk, retrieved a white banner, and handed it to Kurt. "Please lay this across the first five seats in the first row for you, Mrs. Seidenberg and her group. I want you two in front," the rabbi said.

Kurt took the banner, left the office and placed it across the first five seats in the first row, wondering why he wanted them in front. Then, he treaded slowly out toward the rear, searching for Sadie. He had a knot the size of a fist in his stomach, his feet ached from wearing Tony's tapered shoes, and his head throbbed as he watched the worshippers filing into the synagogue. Noting the expressions of awe on their faces as they admired the mural, he felt light-headed.

Kurt was eager to see Rebecca. Sure, he had lusted after Karin since he was fourteen and felt that he was madly in love with her for the last six years, but it was always *Sturm und Drang*. With Rebecca it was different. He felt as if he had fought his way through the jungle, crisscrossing through dense and impenetrable vegetation and then discovered a welcomed clearing, which was sunny and calm.

He spotted Sadie, Rebecca, Leon and Mrs. Feingold in the back, searching for seats. Sadie's right arm was untethered, and as he hurried up the center aisle toward them, Sadie smiled and waved her newly freed arm.

"Congratulations, Mrs. Seidenberg. I'm so happy your arm has been emancipated," he said, shaking her right hand.

"Oh yes, we got back from the doctor hours ago and I keep trying to do things with my left hand and then I remember I can now use my right hand. I'm so *farmisht*."

"Everybody follow me. The rabbi wants us all to sit together in the front row. I saved several seats," he said and led them forward. Sadie pointed backward with her cane.

"What's with the TV cameras?" Sadie said.

"They're from a local cable TV station. They're going to film the renovated interior and the rabbi's sermon."

"*Oy vey*, now the whole city will see our restored mural."

"Yes, that's what I'm afraid of. It's making me very nervous," he said, placing his hand on her shoulder. "I'm so sorry your son couldn't be here tonight."

"What? How did you know that?"

Kurt looked at Rebecca, a sudden panic. Just when things were going so well, he had stepped in *scheisse* again. Talking to Sadie always felt like he was walking in a minefield. Nothing got past her.

"Well, he's obviously not here. Unless he's arriving later," Kurt said.

"No, he couldn't be here, he's a hotsy-totsy lawyer. He has more important things to do—meetings in Washington D.C.," Sadie said, appearing as if she had a sudden case of heartburn.

Mrs. Feingold grabbed Kurt's hand. "I love what you and Sadie have done to our synagogue. It's so very beautiful. It's like stepping into a museum. I can't even believe it."

Leon shook Kurt's hand. "Congratulations, Kurt, you're a very talented painter. And I never even knew that Sadie was interested in art. She only has photographs in her place."

Sadie shrugged, her face as flushed as Kurt's.

"What are you two so worried about? You did an amazing job,"

Rebecca said, glancing at Kurt. They smiled at each other affection-ately.

Kurt could see Sadie from the corner of his eye looking at them with suspicious eyes, but she remained silent.

They stopped at the first row. Kurt gathered up the white banner, and his group settled in their seats. He felt as if he was about to step out of a plane with a potentially faulty parachute. The chute might open at the right time and then again it might not. He was in unchart-ed territory.

Rebecca helped Sadie slip out of her puffy coat, revealing what the old lady was wearing: a pair of black velour pants and a matching V neck top with gold trimming. He'd never seen her wear anything this nice.

Kurt watched Rabbi Feldman as he stepped up to the podium and felt a flourish of anxiety. The rabbi opened the Old Testament and began to speak.

"God gave Solomon wisdom, understanding and largeness of heart. Solomon said, 'David, my father, could not build a temple for the Lord because there were wars all about him. But now the Lord has given me peace on every side, so I will build a temple for the Lord, my God.' Solomon built the temple. He assembled the congregation of Israel and cried out to the Lord, I have built you a house to dwell in forever."

Rabbi Feldman peered out at his congregation with a grave ex-pression on his face. "We, too, built a temple. But it was desecrated . . . not by wars, but by prejudice, ignorance and defiled by hate."

The rabbi studied the faces to his left and focused on a young man in his twenties in the first row. Kurt turned and followed the rabbi's gaze. The young man's eyes were glazed, his lips pursed. He easily relat-ed to the fury the young man was feeling. Kurt too had been enraged when he first saw the defilement of the synagogue, and he's not even Jewish.

"As I look out among our members tonight, I see traces of hatred and seeds of anger in some."

The rabbi then leaned forward and spotted a row of elderly members to his right. "I also see the pain and sadness stamped on the faces of others."

Kurt remembered the expression on Sadie's face when she first entered the synagogue and saw the blood red swastikas, red paint drippings and vile anti-Semitic slogans plastered all over the mural. She appeared horrified, shaken to her core. It frightened him to see this tough old woman, his adversary at the time, diminished like that.

Rabbi Feldman studied other people in the center. "And in some members, I see a thirst for revenge that is marked on their faces. An eye for an eye, so it says in the Book of Exodus, Verse 21. Yet, we have to ask ourselves will hate and violence be stopped by more hate and violence? If we are truly honest with ourselves, we know that isn't the answer. Just look around the world today and you know it hasn't worked so far. It just makes matters worse—much worse," the rabbi said and leaned over the podium.

"Violence begets violence. It always has and it always will. But we cannot help but pose the question, will it ever stop—the bigotry, the cruelty, the bloodshed? Is there a light at the end of this hopelessly dark tunnel?"

He paused for a moment and scanned the walls of the auditorium. The congregation followed his gaze.

"Yet tonight as we look at our restored synagogue, we cannot help but feel pride and joy and relish its beauty, and I want to thank all the members of our synagogue who participated in the lobby and interior cleanup: priming and painting. Those of you who contributed their time and effort, will you please stand up and face everyone."

Several young men and women stood up. The congregation applauded. The rabbi paused again and stared at the mural with his audience following his gaze.

"As you admire our beautifully restored mural, you might want to know who is responsible for this *mitzvah*, a job more than well done. Actually, we can thank an unlikely twosome. Our own Sadie Seidenberg, although temporarily disabled, managed to contribute more than her share as our art director, and Kurt Lichter, who some of you might not know. Kurt is a volunteer from a German peace organization, Project Remembrance, who works with our Jewish seniors. Yes, it was Kurt's country that was responsible for the Holocaust: the brutal slaughter of six million Jews. And yet this young man chose to work here, among us Jews, work with survivors of that monstrous blight on humanity and renovate a desecrated Jewish house of worship."

Kurt feared that this might happen—that he would be singled out in front of the whole congregation. He could barely contain his anxiety. His headache intensified, reaching a new level of pain.

The rabbi gestured to Kurt and Sadie. "Sadie, Kurt, will you please stand up and face everyone."

Kurt and Rebecca assisted Sadie from either side. Kurt helped her turn around and held onto her arm. His face was now a bright red. All eyes were on him. Countless smiling faces filled him with a sense of fulfillment he never thought possible.

The rousing round of applause rang in his ears. He felt a bit woozy as if he had rubber legs and had to hold onto Sadie for support. When the clapping ended, they both sat down.

"So you see, there might be a light at the end of the tunnel after all. If a young German and an elderly Jewish Holocaust survivor can join forces, put aside their ancient differences and restore a violated work of Jewish art, then maybe, just maybe, tolerance among the world's many races and religions is foreseeable in some future time, maybe not in my lifetime, but perhaps for a future generation. And, this very thought makes me want to cry out to our God. Lord, we have built you a house to dwell in forever. Let us recite the *Birkat Shalom*: A Prayer for Peace, first in English and then in Hebrew."

The congregation followed in their prayer books and recited along with Rabbi Feldman.

"Let the day dawn when peace will prevail. O God, Source of peace, lead us to a time when justice and mercy will guide all human endeavor."

Kurt recited the prayer in a voice that came from so deep within him, he didn't recognize it.

After the service ended, Kurt, with Rebecca's assistance, helped Sadie to her feet. Kurt dug around the floor for Sadie's cane, quickly found it and then handed it to her.

Kurt and Rebecca gazed at each other and smiled as they reached the aisle. Sadie looked at Kurt first, and then at Rebecca. He caught the wary expression on her face and knew that Sadie had deduced that he and her granddaughter were more than just friends, even though they had tried their best to conceal it.

"Is there something I should know about here?" Sadie asked, cocking her head to one side, her eyes narrowed, focusing on her granddaughter.

"Grandma, don't worry," Rebecca said, taking her hand.

"Worry is my middle name. I just hope you know what you're doing."

They followed behind Leon as he wheeled Mrs. Feingold up the aisle into the lobby. He and Sadie were received as if they were triumphant heroes. Everyone showered them with praise for their brilliantly restored mural.

David rushed up to Kurt and wrapped his arm around his shoulders as they reached the lobby.

"I said to shape up or ship out, but I had no idea you would become . . . well . . . such a *mensch*."

"A *mensch*?"

David nodded, smiling. "It's a Yiddish expression to describe a decent, responsible, admirable person."

"*Mensch* is also a German word, but it means a human being, a person," Kurt said.

"Well, Jews added more to the meaning. We like to embellish. It's a genetic trait."

As they walked into the lobby, he spotted Rabbi Feldman in a huddle with Sadie, Rebecca, Leon and Mrs. Feingold. The rabbi was speaking, and they hung on his every word. He couldn't hear what the rabbi was saying, but then Rebecca turned her head, noticed Kurt and waved him over. Maybe she sensed him near, he thought, and headed toward them.

The rabbi took Sadie's hand and smiled at Kurt. "So, Sadela, was I right about this young man?" Rabbi Feldman said.

Sadie stared at Kurt with a critical eye, teasingly. "Hmmm, perhaps you were."

Kurt watched Sadie's expression change from mischievous to reflective. When they first met, she would stare at him as if she had a foul taste in her mouth. Now, her expression was warm, sweet—like she was genuinely fond of him.

Rebecca threw her arm around Sadie's shoulder and squeezed her, smiling fondly at her grandmother, who smiled back in kind.

He studied their faces, grandmother and granddaughter, centering on their facial features, took a mental snapshot and felt an urge to capture the two generations of Jewish women to be remembered always.

Kurt strutted into the YHMA lobby and approached the front desk victoriously. This was a brand new feeling for him, and he reveled in it. Tony was on duty, and he greeted Kurt with a laugh.

"Hey, Michelangelo—nice duds. They look better on you than on me."

He gaped at Kurt's head, amused. "Or is it Rabbi Michelangelo?"

Kurt stared at him curiously for a moment and then felt the top of his head. Both embarrassed and surprised, he removed the yarmulke.

"If you told me six months ago I'd be attending a service in a synagogue surrounded on all sides by Jews, praised by their rabbi, called a *mensch* and would make friends with an old Jewish lady and fall in love with her granddaughter, I would have probably wiped the fucking floor with you."

"Well, color me lucky, I didn't even know you six months ago."

Kurt smiled at his friend and then walked toward the elevator, catching one immediately. His feet were now numb from the pain he endured for the past several hours. He pressed his number and his mind jumped to Rabbi Feldman's sermon that encapsulated the essence of what was wrong with humankind: the capacity for hate and prejudice in one group of people toward another. What made humans have such a predilection to despise others because of their nationality, race or religion: all accidents of birth? The differences rather than the similarities. He guessed that it probably had to do with the theoretical Darwinian fight for survival and the apparent need for one group to feel superior than the other to make up for their own inadequacies. Was it instinctual or learned? It must be in our DNA, he concluded. There could be no other explanation for it.

Yet, the rabbi's conclusion implied that if all human beings accepted the truth that we are all members of the same species, underneath all the trappings of our outward appearance and birthright, we're much more alike than we are different. And, if we can work together to make our planet a more livable and peaceful place, we can replace hate with respect, fondness and perhaps love. Who knows?

His mind then skipped to Rebecca, her beautiful smile, her adoration toward her grandmother, to Sadie's joyful pride in their mural, and almost missed his floor. He barely escaped the elevator door closing on him.

He rushed to his room, opened the door and kicked off his shoes, wriggling his toes to revive the feeling back. He then peeled off his jacket, gently placing it on his bed and folded the yarmulke neatly in half, pressing it down with his hands to prevent it from wrinkling as if it were a priceless treasure. He wasted no time changing into his jeans and tee shirt.

Kurt stared at his sketchbook and the box of pastel sticks on top of his small desk. He picked up the sketchbook and sat in the desk chair and closed his eyes. He imagined Rebecca's beautiful face—her large brown eyes with a hint of green and how he was mesmerized by her gaze, her full, perfectly shaped lips and her long, flowing, reddish-brown hair.

He pictured Sadie with her wise eyes and wrinkled, expressive face. Every line proclaiming that she had been through hell and back, but lived to tell the tale.

He opened the pad, flipped to a clean page, opened the box of pastels and took out a henna colored stick and began to draw Rebecca. He started with her hair, creating wavy lines with the tip and then turned it on its side to create volume and waves. He used his finger, shading in the empty spaces.

He opened the desk drawer, removed a charcoal pencil and with its sharpened point drew her eyes. He switched from using the pencil to the pastel sticks to produce the contrast of pigment tone in the pupils. He then outlined the rest of Rebecca's face with the pencil and then did the same to Sadie's face.

He continued to work into the night, paying particular attention to the warmth of Rebecca's smile, and attempting to capture Sadie's indomitable spirit.

Chapter 30

Kurt knocked on Sadie's apartment door several times. He held a large package wrapped in brown butcher paper, shifting the unwieldy package from one hand to the other and once again heard the familiar sound of Sadie's cane thumping on the door and her shouting that she'll be right there.

At last, Sadie appeared, a welcoming smile on her face, wearing her black velour pants with a black and white striped boat-neck sweater, looking rather stylish. She apparently dressed for this occasion.

"You're a couple of minutes early. I was just getting our brunch ready. Come in," she said.

"Sorry, I didn't want to be late," Kurt said.

"No, no, it's fine, no need to apologize," she said, leading him into the living room. "Sit, sit. We'll have brunch in here, buffet style," she said, leading him into the living room. Kurt made his way toward the couch, catching a glimpse of the food awaiting him on the coffee table: smoked salmon and cream cheese bagel sandwiches, plates, napkins, a vintage china tea set and a wooden box packed with assorted flavored tea bags.

Sadie gestured with her cane to the package under his arm. "What do you have there?"

"A surprise for you."

"For me? What is it? It looks like it's maybe a picture," she said, her eyes lit with the enthusiasm of a small child.

Kurt placed her present on the overstuffed chair across from the coffee table, and then he sat on the faded flowered couch. He'd only seen her living room in passing. Her couch, seemingly decades old, was very comfortable, embracing him as he eased his body into it.

"You'll just have to open it and see," Kurt said, smiling playfully. He reveled at how quickly she ripped off the paper and at the look of amazement on her face when she unveiled his pastel drawing of her and Rebecca in a thin black metal frame. He had captured something he'd only recently perceived: the matching smiles on their faces. It wasn't until Kurt was working on the drawing that he realized the marked similarities between the two despite their difference in age.

Kurt's heart was beating fast. Joy did this to him. He was so unaccustomed to it.

"Oh, I really love this. It's so beautiful. You're a good boy. It's the best present I've received in a long time. I can't believe how you were able to capture us so perfectly, even how much we love each other."

She stared at the bottom of the drawing.

"You didn't sign this picture. You have to sign it. An artist should always sign his own work."

"Oh, I didn't want to spoil it with my name plastered on it."

"No, no, no, please sign it, just on the bottom, in small letters."

"Okay, I'll do it for you."

Kurt pulled out a nearly spent charcoal pencil from his pocket, kneeled down in front of the drawing and wrote his name on the very bottom.

"Thank you, thank you so much. I'm *kvelling!*"

"You're welcome and ah, yes, like the German word *quellen.*"

"Now, let's eat. I'm starving. Do you like lox?"

"Oh yes, I love *lachs*. In Germany we eat it on toast or black bread."

"Here we eat it with a smear of cream cheese on bagels. It's my favorite meal," she said, gesturing to the food. "Help yourself. *Ess gezunterhait!*"

"Ah, *essen bei guter gesundheit,*" Kurt said, taking a plate. He picked up a bagel sandwich and began eating.

Sadie sat down next to him and grabbed one for herself, biting into it immediately. She noticed a dab of cream cheese on Kurt's chin and handed him a napkin.

"Here, wipe the *schmutz* off of your chin," she said, pointing to her chin.

Kurt laughed and did as Sadie recommended. "Yes, *schmutz*. Yiddish and German are very similar."

"Yiddish is kind of a mixture of Hebrew and German. My father was born in Poland and my mother was born in Germany. They both knew how to speak German, but we mainly spoke Yiddish in the house and with our friends. Today only the *Alta Kachers* still speak it."

Kurt paused and gazed at Sadie for a minute.

"I want to thank you, Mrs. Seidenberg."

"Me? For what?"

"For helping me get back to my painting."

She paused for a moment. Her eyebrows raised as if she was deep in thought. "Once an artist, always an artist. It's in your blood, in your soul."

"When did you first start to draw?" Kurt said.

*   *   *

Sadie put her plate down on the table and turned toward Kurt. She was somewhat hesitant to share that part of her life with him. She had kept so much of it a secret all these years, but she perceived genuine curiosity in his eyes and felt a deep fondness for him.

"My father had a shop in Berlin, Teitlebaum's Scheiderei, near *Oranienburger Strasse . . .*"

"Oh yes, I learned in school that area was once mainly Jewish. They've even restored the Neue Synagogue on *Oranienburger Strasse* and now that area has many art galleries and studios. I hung out there all the time."

Images of her father's large, busy tailor shop before Hitler rushed to Sadie's mind, and she visualized the bustling street with shoppers hurrying in all directions.

"We had a cozy little home in back of the shop. My father and my brother Leo took care of the customers, and my father and my mother altered the clothes. I used to watch my mother fit the customers, and I would draw them on the sketchpad my father bought me for my eleventh birthday. It was very large and the paper was a very good quality. My little sister, Esther, would curl up at my side. The customers loved to see the sketches of themselves. They made such a big fuss over me. Sometimes they would even give me a few coins as a tip, which I used to buy my pencils and charcoal sticks. My parents were so proud of their little Sadela, that was what they called me. My father said I would go to the university to study art, if they had to sew a million suits to get me there."

"Did you go? What happened?"

Sadie knew that Kurt was enjoying hearing about her past and about Germany before Hitler, from the high-pitched tone of his voice and the intense expression on his face.

"What happened? First the depression and then Adolph Hitler, that's what happened."

As if it was yesterday, Sadie's mind flashed back to 1938, the deserted streets, all of the shops boarded up, including Teitlebaum's. Germany after *Krystallnacht*. She still remembered that night when shattered glass swirled like snowflakes all over Berlin. Nazi graffiti now marred her father's once-thriving shop. S.S. sirens reverberated incessantly, assaulting the ears.

"It first started when Hitler became Chancellor of Germany. Anti-Semitism was spreading across Germany like wildfire. It became harder and harder for Jews to live a normal life. We didn't have the same rights as we had before and we couldn't go to the universities. Brownshirt youths invaded the streets, intimidating everyone. It was terrifying. My mother's sister, Sylvia, begged my mother for us to flee with her family to England. Her husband had relatives in New York and they had the money and connections to flee Germany, but my father loved his shop too much and insisted that soon things would get better. But, it didn't. It got worse. Much worse. By then I was twelve. Esther was nine and Leo was sixteen."

"I read about *Krystallnacht* in grade school. The teacher showed us pictures. Even synagogues were destroyed. It was terrible," Kurt said.

"It was like an earthquake. The sound of glass shattering echoed in my ears for weeks after. Our beautiful shop ruined, with swastikas painted all over the front. The Brownshirts threw cans of red paint inside everywhere. We cleaned it up the best we could and boarded up the front of the shop. We hid in the back, scared to death. We had nowhere else to go. My mother and father looked like they aged twenty years from worrying so much. It was too late to escape Germany. The Schulzes, who owned a jewelry shop next to ours, helped us by sneaking in food and anything else we needed."

"Oh, were they Germans?" Kurt asked.

"Yes, they were. We knew them for many years, and they were very kind to us. Not all Germans were Nazis and some of them were sympathetic to Jews, even risking their own lives to protect their Jewish friends," she said and noticed Kurt's face softening a bit when he heard that not all Germans were monsters.

"But, we all knew that any day something very terrible would happen. Then one morning, it did. All of a sudden, while we were eating our breakfast, four S.S. officers marched to the back entrance and pounded on our boarded up door. They forced their way into our kitchen with a battering ram and rounded us up like criminals. I knew I couldn't take anything but a small suitcase. I only wanted my art things..."

"Did they let you, did they let you take them?" Kurt leaned into Sadie, moved by her story.

"No, no, they didn't. I scrambled to get them—my charcoals and water colors, but a trooper grabbed me before I could. They dragged us into the back of a truck and drove us to the Grunewald train station. We barely survived the ride to Auschwitz."

She moved away from him, recalling the horrific images of the Nazi soldiers savagely beating thousands of Jews into lines and then herding them onto the trains. The words came pouring out of her. She didn't even know from where. She never told her story to anyone before, except for bits and pieces to Rabbi Feldman.

"They packed us into the trains so tightly we couldn't breathe and you wouldn't believe the smell. I'm sure you've seen movies and documentaries showing these Nazi trains jammed with Jews like they were animals."

"Yes, yes, I have... so brutal," Kurt said, wincing.

"It was a million times more terrible in real life. Then, when we arrived they carted us off the train with the butts of their rifles. Esther,

Leo and I held onto our mother and father for dear life. Leo had to prop my poor father up. He had gotten so frail from the ride, while Esther and I helped our mother, who now walked with a noticeable limp from being squashed into the train. The guards shoved Leo and my father into the men's line. Esther and I managed to hold onto our mother and then we were all pushed into the women's line. They threw us onto trucks and took us to the camp."

Sadie paused for a moment. These horrific memories that she kept hidden for so many years gushed to the surface. The agonized faces of the women holding their screeching babies in their quaking arms, their eyes revealing what all of them felt on that train to hell. Sadie remembered how vulnerable she felt staring at her *muter aun foter* and thinking that for the first time in her young life her parents could do nothing to protect her, Esther and Leo. A train full of powerless people at the mercy of their evil captors.

"When we got to Auschwitz, we searched for Leo and our father in the men's lines, but we didn't see them. There were so many men. Esther and I held onto my mother because she couldn't stand up on her own. Then an S.S. trooper came over, sized up the situation and grabbed our mother away from us. It was obvious they eliminated the frail ones. We tried so hard to grasp onto her, but we just weren't strong enough. We wailed as he dragged her into the line of old women, where she collapsed to the ground the minute he let go of her. The guard yelled, '*sich aufrichten*' several times and when she didn't get up, he shouted for a doctor, who immediately took her pulse. He shook his head and said '*sie est tot*.' We didn't know what happened to her. She just laid there on the cold ground with the doctor and S.S. officer staring at her dead body, obviously disgusted at yet another pathetic, feeble Jew."

She stopped talking, the image of her mother falling to her death overwhelmed her. Whether it was a stroke or a heart attack or simply an inability to suffer one more indignity, she never knew.

Tears streamed down Sadie's anguished face. She used her hand to wipe them away. Kurt moved closer to her. She stared at his watery eyes; the color was drained out of his face. He picked up a napkin off the table. "I am so sorry, so sorry, Mrs. Seidenberg," he said, handing it to her.

She blotted her eyes with the napkin and tried to regain her composure.

"And your father and Leo?" Kurt said softly, almost whispering.

"I never saw them again. I tried to find them after the war but couldn't. They were probably both killed in the crematorium the day we arrived. My father was too old to work, too old to keep alive, and my brother most likely wouldn't allow himself to be separated from him."

"And Esther?"

Sadie eyes shrunk smaller, her face tightened. She couldn't bear uttering another word.

She held up her hand. "Enough. Enough about the past," she pleaded.

Kurt took Sadie's hand in his and held it tightly.

Chapter 31

Kurt hiked up the subway steps, emerging onto Lexington Avenue and Ninety-second Street. He couldn't shake Sadie's story from his mind. The weight of it made him wobbly.

The sun was setting, and the street lamps switched on as he approached the YMHA entrance. He spotted Karin pacing back and forth like a cat staking out its territory. Several people entering the building had to swerve around her to avoid a collision. When he got nearer, she hurried to him with outstretched arms. She appeared genuinely happy to see him. The feeling was not mutual. He pulled away.

"Sorry I'm late. What happened? Your message sounded so urgent."

"You haven't called me in such a long time," she said, pouting like a hurt child the way she always did when she was displeased with his behavior.

"I've been very busy, Karin. Very busy," he said, his voice quivering, his mind still reeling.

"With what? Are you still working with the Jews?" she said, punctuating the word "Jews" in an edgy tone.

"Yes, I am. The synagogue near the Seniors Outreach Center was *vandalisiert* by some hate group, probably neo-Nazis. They have them here too. It was terrible. I've been helping restore their beautiful mural. Such a big job."

"Oh, I see."

She moved closer to him. "Aren't you going to invite me up to your room?"

"No, no. It is much too small for two people. Let's not talk here, so many people going in and out. Come, let's take a walk," he said, catching a whiff of her heavy perfume. His nose was not accustomed to her smell any more.

He steered her toward the corner of Ninety-second Street and Lexington Avenue where they stopped for the light. She turned and gazed at him with heavy-lidded eyes. He knew exactly what that expression meant. She was actually trying to seduce him after she threw him out on his ass and broke his heart. He couldn't fucking believe it.

"I've been thinking about you a lot, Kurt. I've been missing you so much. I thought you and . . ."

The light changed and they crossed the street heading north on Lexington Avenue. Most of the local shops were closing up for the night and foot traffic was light, except for a few people walking their dogs.

"You want me back? Now?" he said, stunned. His voice raised an octave, causing a small black poodle trotting by on a leash to yelp frantically.

She turned to Kurt and gently caressed his face with a pathetic look in her eyes, the disingenuous way she would always look at him when she wanted her own way. In a way he pitied her. Her conniving, scheming ways always got her what she wanted, but not this time, this time those ways would work against her wishes.

Kurt walked to the corner of Ninety-third Street toward Third

Avenue, a quieter, more residential street. Karin followed, hastening to keep up with him.

"Suddenly you show up and I should forget everything. Christ! What about your new boyfriend?" he asked, but knew her professor probably dumped her, otherwise she wouldn't have turned up out of the blue.

"That's all over now,"

"What happened?"

"It doesn't matter. I've always loved you, Kurt. You know that. Since we were kids," she said, linking her arm through his and trying to sound sincere, which for her was always difficult.

"It's different now. I'm different. Things have changed," he said, removing her arm.

"What? What things have changed? You mean you met someone else?"

Kurt took a deep breath to gather his thoughts. He was not sure how to explain to Karin all that had happened to him since he saw her last. He couldn't believe how clearly he saw her now.

She had never really loved him for who he was as a person, his thoughts, his beliefs, the core of his being, of that he was now sure. What she loved about him was just superficial—the way they looked together, like perfectly matched bookends. She was the one who taught him how to make love. It wasn't something he discovered on his own, developing his own way. It was her way, the way that would give her the most pleasure. Never mind about him. It was hard to believe that he actually ever loved her and that there was a time when he would have done anything to please her.

Kurt had been on his own for only a few months, yet it seemed like a lifetime ago when he lived with Karin, his one true love. Funny how that can happen. You think that you can't live without someone, and then something happens within you, and you can't imagine how you ever loved that person in the first place.

"Yes, there is someone new, but it's more than that. I thought you dumping me and being stuck here with the Jews would be the death of me. Instead, it has been just the opposite."

"What do you mean?"

Kurt spotted a brownstone with wide, clean steps and stopped in front of them.

"Let's sit here for awhile," he said. He gestured for Karin to sit next to him, which she did, reluctantly.

He could tell from her face that she was bewildered, a new expression for her. She was always the one in control, dangling him around like a marionette.

"Karin, do you ever think about the past?"

"The past? What past?"

"The Nazis. The war."

"What are you talking about? I don't understand what you're asking me."

"Do you ever think about what our grandfathers did in the war?"

"No, not really. I suppose they were soldiers fighting the war in Russia or France somewhere."

"How do you know that? My grandfather never talked to me once about the war, even when I asked. I don't know what the fuck he did then. Was he an S.S. trooper? Was he a guard in the concentration camps? Did he assist in those horrific medical experiments?"

"I don't fucking know what they did and I don't fucking care," she said. "What difference does it make now? It was years and years ago. Most of those people are dead now anyway. I want to talk about us. We are alive."

"They're not all dead, Karin. Some of them survived. The old lady

I've been helping since I've been here survived, and we have a good relationship now," he said and swiveled toward her. "I've been thinking about my family, my neighbors, the old ones on my street where I grew up and the part they played in the war. Did they send people to the camps? Did they gas them? Did they kill mothers, fathers, children? Did they hide any Jews or do anything to help them? Maybe it doesn't make any difference now, except that same blood is in me. It matters to me."

Karin glared at him as if he were a stranger.

"Isn't this typical of you, finding misery wherever you go. Why is it so difficult for you just to be happy?"

"That's just it, Karin, I am happy."

What he didn't say was, I'm happy without you. I'm happy because I can paint again, because I've met someone truly wonderful. But she must have heard it anyway, because she stood up, and without saying another word, walked away.

Kurt watched her hurrying down the street toward Second Avenue and felt cleansed. He rose and sauntered back toward Lexington Avenue, but instead of heading back to the Y, he got the sudden urge to see Rebecca. He trotted toward the downtown bus stop.

He sat in a window seat and, as the streets whizzed by, scenes of Sadie's life in Germany before and after Hitler flashed in front of him. He reflected on how in a relatively short time her life changed from hopeful to dreadful. One day she was a happy girl surrounded by her loving family, laughing, drawing, living a normal life and then suddenly it was all gone. He couldn't imagine how she was able to endure that amount of tragedy, being ripped apart from her family, being systemically starved to death, living in the most appalling conditions possible, and then continue on living. It mystified him. He had spent most of his young life lamenting about one thing or another, but in truth it was all over nothing. Nothing at all in comparison.

Skipping ahead to his encounter with Karin, he never thought there would come a time when he would no longer need and want her. Her resistance to confronting the Holocaust and Germany's past horrors appalled him. She might as well have denied that it ever happened. But, it occurred to him that just a few months ago, he would have had the same reaction as her, if he were asked the same questions. He never gave a fuck about the Holocaust and its victims; he never gave them a second thought.

The bus stopped and he looked out the window. Christ, it was Rebecca's street. He jumped up and rang the bell. The doors opened and he leaped out.

He hurried to Rebecca's building, exchanged smiles and "hellos" with the doorman and entered the building. He knocked several times on Rebecca's door, hoping she was home. He had so much to tell her. He saw her peeking through the peephole and was relieved she was there. He waited a couple of minutes before the door opened.

"Oh, Kurt, is there something wrong?"

"No, nothing. Sorry, but I just had to see you. Are you busy?" Kurt said.

He heard a commanding male voice. "Rebecca? Rebecca, who's there?"

Rebecca shouted back, "A friend. I'll be back in a minute."

She gently placed her hand over Kurt's mouth, quickly moved him into the hallway and closed the door behind her.

Kurt was shocked to hear a man's voice. "Who's that?"

"My father. He arrived a couple of days ago," she said softly, almost whispering. "Are you sure you're okay?"

Kurt caressed her hair, held her face and kissed her tenderly. He followed her lead and answered quietly, "I am now, I just needed to see you."

"I'm glad you did. My father isn't the easiest person to be around. I should get back."

Still facing Kurt, she opened the door slightly. Jack Seidenberg's booming voice interrupted them. "Rebecca, why don't you invite your friend in?"

"Why don't I go in? For just a minute."

"Not now, not yet," Rebecca said and called out to her father, "My friend can't stay now, Daddy."

He sensed that Rebecca was holding something back from him, she seemed guarded, almost frightened.

She kissed Kurt quickly but sweetly. "You can meet him another time. I really need to get back, we were in the middle of dinner."

"Okay, I'll see you soon," Kurt said.

"Yes, call me tomorrow."

Kurt pulled Rebecca into another kiss. He smiled, turned and stepped toward the elevator with Rebecca's kiss lingering on his lips, swathed in her sweet lavender scent.

Rebecca slowly walked back to the dining table, dreading her overbearing father's questions. She sat down across from him, detecting the suspicion in his eyes.

"Which friend was that?" Jack said.

"It was just a friend, Emily . . . from school . . ."

"Oh, and she couldn't come in for a minute to say hello?"

"No, Daddy, she couldn't. She had to be somewhere else and this is my apartment, not a courtroom, so could you please stop cross-examining me?"

"Okay, okay."

Jack picked up his wine glass and took a sip, then hastily put it down. "I've been meaning to ask you and I keep forgetting, has Josh Goodman called you yet?"

Rebecca hoped he wouldn't ask this question. She swirled the food around in her plate with her fork the way she did as a child to appear that she was busy eating. Josh had called her weeks ago, but she blew him off as she never had any intention of going on a blind date with a guy her father had fixed her up with, especially since he sounded like some egotistical kid. He talked incessantly about himself and how he was the youngest person who ever made law review at Columbia. That was the extent of their conversation.

"Who has time to date? I told you I was too busy with school."

"Oh, really, you're that busy?"

By the look on her father's face she knew her father wasn't buying it, but that was his problem, not hers.

"Yes, I am. I'm that busy and I'm old enough to choose who I want to have dinner with."

Rebecca perceived the mistrust and disappointment in her father's face, but refused to feel guilty about it.

Chapter 32

Sadie hiked up the window shade allowing the late morning sun to illuminate her kitchen. She hobbled over to the counter and cut the red and white string off of the pink Moishe's Bakery box and removed her favorite pastries, *rugelach,* a variety of the delicious miniature pastries, heavily favoring the cheese and chocolate, placing them in a big china bowl. She set the bowl and a stack of paper napkins on a sterling silver tray, which was a wedding present from her Cousin Yettie. Yettie had moved to Florida several years ago to the assisted living place that her son, Jack, would like her to live in. She carried the tray into the living room and put it on the coffee table, and then hurried back into the kitchen to get the cups and saucers.

She moved around faster now that she had a high stabilizer fracture boot on her leg from the fancy Upper East Side orthopedist, the one her son had insisted on and took her to a couple of days ago.

A loud knocking on her door indicated that her punctual, impatient son and her granddaughter had arrived. There was nothing gentle about Jack. While most people knocked on a door gently, he pounded.

"I'm coming, I'm coming…"

She heard Rebecca's voice call back, "Take your time, Grandma. There's no rush." Sadie pictured Rebecca's eyes rolling contemptuously at her father for being so needlessly intolerant. Only after she had brought the china to the living room and set them on the coffee table, did she move toward the door.

Sadie let them in and led them into the living room. "Come in and enjoy the best *rugelach* in New York City."

Sadie and Rebecca sat down on the couch, while Jack eased into the matching arm chair.

"I'm telling you, Mom, this neighborhood is getting worse every year. I checked with the police department and the crime rate has gone up seven percent in this complex alone. There's always garbage on the floor in the lobby, the elevator reeked of urine, and your apartment is in dire need of a new paint job. There are so many cracks in the ceiling, I'm afraid it's going to fall on your head. I still have your name on the waiting list for Palms Village. For God's sake, Mom . . ."

"You worry too much, Jack. Besides, it's too sunny in Florida, I'll get melanoma." She smacked her lips as she stuffed a miniature pastry into her mouth. "Eat, all ready, before I finish them up. I bet you can't get *rugelach* like this in Los Angeles."

Sadie loved teasing her son about the many virtues of New York City as compared to Los Angeles. It was like a running gag between them, particularly when it came to Jewish and Chinese food.

Jack picked one up, took a small bite and then devoured it whole. "You're right, Mom, we can't. These are definitely out of this world," he conceded.

Sadie gazed at the coffee table and started to rise. "Oh, I forgot to bring in the tea."

"Sit, Grandma. I'll go and get it," Rebecca said and rushed out of the room.

Sadie noticed Jack gazing down at Kurt's pastel drawing of her and Rebecca propped up against the wall across from where they were sitting. Oh my God. What had she done now? She couldn't believe that she actually forgot to remove that picture from the living room. Old age is a curse! She had deliberately put off hanging it up until after Jack went back to L.A. Her age was showing more and more each day. Lately, she felt like she was holding onto her sanity by a thread. She knew exactly what was coming next.

"Who did that?" Jack said, pointing to the picture.

"Who did what?"

"The framed drawing over against that wall. It wasn't there the last time I was here."

"Oh, that picture. No one you know. Have another *rugelach*, try the chocolate," Sadie said, trying her best to sound casual.

Jack picked up the napkin off of his lap and carefully wiped the pastry crumbs off his face and shirt. He stepped over to the picture, picked it up and held it at arm's length. He studied it for a few minutes.

"It's quite good. A remarkable likeness. It seems like the artist knows both of you very well. He or she was able to capture your personalities as well as your features. Extraordinary."

Rebecca returned to the living room with the tea pot, witnessed her father holding Kurt's drawing and glanced over to her grandmother, whose face was flushed.

He moved the picture closer to him, noticed the signature at the bottom and read it out loud.

"Kurt Lichter . . . Kurt Lichter? He did this?"

Rebecca tiptoed over to the coffee table, set the teapot down and sat on the couch next to Sadie.

"Good, isn't he?" Sadie said and turned to Rebecca for help.

"You don't know him, Daddy. He's the boy from that peace organization who's been helping Grandma. I told you about him a while
ago. He helped restore the mural in the synagogue with Grandma."

"You said some boy from some community group was helping my
mother. You never mentioned his name."

Jack put the picture down and marched over to the chair and sat.
He turned and faced Sadie.

"Kurt Lichter? That's the German boy you warned me about. The
boy you said was after my Rebecca."

Sadie nodded, shamefaced. She was the one who had made Kurt
sign his drawing. "Yes, yes, I did. But, there's nothing to worry about
now, Jack. I was mistaken. He's a good, sweet boy and a wonderful
artist, and he's been very helpful to me. He took me to the doctors, to
the synagogue. We had a rocky beginning, but that was more my fault
than his. You should see what he accomplished in the synagogue. I can
take you there. You can see for yourself."

"Mother, what's going on here? You told me that you didn't know
where Rebecca met him, and now it appears that she met him here
through you," Jack said, leaning forward, staring directly into his
mother's eyes.

Sadie raised her voice up a notch. "What? You think I fixed them
up. I don't know what I said. It was months ago. You expect me to
remember everything at my age?"

"Right, you can't remember and I'm not losing my hair."

Sadie peered at Rebecca and spotted a pained expression on her
face. She would do anything to reverse what she did.

Jack shifted his gaze toward his daughter. "Rebecca, what do you
have to say for yourself? Are you or are you not seeing this boy?"

"We're not seeing each other in the way you think. Kurt and I are
just friends. I've never known anyone before from Germany and I find
him very interesting. That's all."

"So that's your story? You're just friends?"

"Jack, stop, stop accusing her of something she's not doing," Sadie said and banged her fist on the table. "Rebecca has been seeing Kurt in my company—mostly at the synagogue when we were working there together. Now let that be the end of it."

Sadie hoped that it would be the end of it, but she knew her son, and she knew it would not.

Chapter 33

It was an unusually warm, breezy day for a New York winter day, permitting Kurt and Rebecca to share a bagged lunch on a bench in front of NYU Medical Center. Kurt swept his hair away from his eyes and took a bite out of his sandwich, fixing his gaze on Rebecca as she bit into an apple. A few days ago she was so edgy about her father being there, she wouldn't even let him into her apartment. It almost seemed that she couldn't wait to get rid of him. This was so unlike her. She was usually so direct. No bullshit, no game playing—these were the qualities he loved in her.

"Why wouldn't you let your father meet me?" he said in a purposely soft, non-confrontational tone.

"Not now, maybe the next time he comes here. He has back-to-back meetings this trip." She took out a cup of coffee from the bag and sipped it slowly. "The truth is my father is extremely over-protective and managerial. He needs to be eased into the idea of meeting you and it has nothing to do with you, I mean, who you are as a person."

Kurt pondered Rebecca's explanation for a moment. "Is it because I'm a *shiksa*?"

Rebecca grinned and caressed his face lovingly. "A *shiksa* is a girl who isn't Jewish. You would be a *shegetz* and my father hasn't liked any of my boyfriends, even the Jewish ones. He and I have totally opposite opinions when it comes to men suitable for me."

He knew she was just being kind and sensed she was holding something back. He finished his sandwich and dropped the aluminum foil wrapper into the brown paper deli bag, while Rebecca gulped down the rest of her coffee and threw the cup into the bag. Kurt slid close to her and pulled her into a long smoldering kiss. "It's just that I'm a different person when I am with you."

"I feel the same way about you, too." She gave him a quick kiss and then checked her watch. "Oh, my anatomy class is in twenty minutes. I wish I was taking your class instead of mine. Grandma told me how much she's been enjoying teaching with you."

Kurt smiled. "Yes, I would like that, too, but I'm afraid you're forty years too young. I better be moving or I'll be late as well."

Kurt hurried into the Jewish Seniors Outreach Center and raced to the conference room.

David called out to him, "You don't have to run. It's okay, Kurt, Mrs. Seidenberg has started the class without you."

"I'm sorry, there was a traffic jam on Second Avenue." It was safe to blame the traffic in Manhattan as it was always a mess. No one would dare contradict you.

Kurt reached the room where a large sign had been Scotch-taped to the wall next to the door: Art Class—Working with Charcoals, Tuesdays at 2:00 p.m., Instructors: Sadie Seidenberg and Kurt Lichter. He read the notice; a rare sense of pride washed over him. At first he had vetoed David's idea. Why the hell would he want to teach a bunch of old people to draw? But David insisted. The class was spurred by several members of the center asking for it, after seeing the magnificent work Kurt and Sadie did restoring their synagogue's defaced mural.

Kurt learned that some of his students had been artists when they were younger, but were now hampered by arthritis, and could no longer manipulate the charcoal sticks. He found that massaging their fingers with Red Tiger Balm, a remedy for muscular and joint pain he found on the internet, helped them handle the sticks easily. With one of his students, Mr. Moscowitz, a man in his mid-90s, Kurt had to guide his trembling hand to complete his renderings.

He actually enjoyed helping his students find or renew their creative spirit and was amazed how patient and supportive he was with them. He never knew he possessed those qualities. At the Arts University the air was heavy with rivalry, each student competing with the other to earn praise from the teachers and when the teachers asked for opinions from classmates, their feedback seemed intentionally mean-spirited.

Kurt stepped into the room, spotted today's subject, a bowl of artificial fruit placed on a small table draped with black velvet, and watched the members of the class working diligently at drawings perched on large wooden easels. He went around the room and checked the status of their work. He was pleased that they were all off to a good start.

He observed Sadie helping Mrs. Feingold, who seemed to be struggling with her drawing. Sadie sat beside her and demonstrated how to hold the piece of charcoal.

"If you hold the charcoal on its side like this, you can shade the orange," she said as she guided Mrs. Feingold's arm. "See how the blending of light and shadows gives it depth?"

"It looks good enough to eat," Mrs. Feingold said.

Kurt moved closer to her drawing. "Mrs. Feingold, you're becoming quite the artist."

She savored Kurt's praise and tapped Sadie on her shoulder. "I owe it all to my good friend here."

Sadie wrapped her arm around her friend's shoulder and gave her a gentle hug. While Mrs. Feingold continued shading, Kurt grabbed a chair and pulled it next to Sadie and sat.

"I'm so sorry I was late. The downtown bus was caught in traffic."

"No problem. David helped with the easels, table and the bowl of fruit."

"That's good. Mrs. Seidenberg, can I ask you something . . . something personal?"

"Personal? How personal?"

"It's about your son, Rebecca's father."

Sadie motioned Kurt to the back of the room for some privacy. "My Jack? What about him?" she said, lowering her voice.

"Do you think he would disapprove of me? I mean for Rebecca. Maybe you could tell him I'm not so bad."

Kurt noticed Sadie's expression change from neutral to concern. "You don't tell Jack anything, you just butt heads."

"Maybe, if he met me, he would change his mind. Rebecca doesn't think it's a good idea, at least not now, but maybe you can talk to him. He might listen to you, his own mother."

Sadie was unable to look Kurt in the face. She bowed her head and shrugged. Kurt deduced that she was as powerless over Jack Seidenberg as Rebecca. Perhaps he was better off not meeting him. He sounded as if he would be a good match for his own father: reliably obstinate.

Chapter 34

Rebecca sat at a small desk off the dining area in her apartment, hovering over an oversized textbook, and highlighted a section on the skeletal system with a yellow marker. She desperately tried to focus on the material as thoughts of Kurt, her father and her grandmother rose to the surface like scuba divers running out of air.

The ringing doorbell jarred Rebecca out of the human anatomy, causing her heart to beat faster. She checked her watch as she wasn't expecting anyone until a half-hour later and headed to the door. She viewed her father, stone-faced, through the peephole and quickly opened it.

"You're early, Daddy. I'm not ready."

"Dinner can wait."

Jack stepped into her apartment, removed his overcoat and placed it on one of the dining chairs. He stood silent for a moment. It was obvious he was furious with her.

"I saw you before . . ."

"What do you mean? When? Where?"

"I saw the two of you this afternoon. You and that boy. It was that German boy, wasn't it?" He snatched his iPhone out of his pants pocket. After a few clicks he showed her a picture of her and Kurt kissing hours earlier in front of NYU Medical Center. "I was going to confront the two of you then and there, but I don't like to make scenes in public, particularly in front of your school."

Her father always was a first-class helicopter parent, intervening in every aspect of her life: school, summer camps, hobbies, girl- and boyfriends. Everything she did he made it his business. But this was the last straw.

"How did you know where I was? Did you have me followed? Were you spying on me?"

Her voice rose an octave. Her face felt like it was burning up as if someone waved a lit match in front of it. She imagined a puff of steam erupting from both ears and the top of her head like one of those angry cartoon characters.

"No, no, of course I wasn't spying on you and no, you're not being followed. My morning meeting ended early and my next meeting wasn't until later. Since I was near the medical center, I remembered you telling me that you had your anatomy class there on Tuesdays and thought I'd take a chance, surprise you and take you to lunch. I spotted you from Second Avenue, and I saw the two of you together carrying on like that. I thought you were going to devour each other. I decided it was best for me to turn back and confront you later rather than in front of that boy. The worst part of it is that you lied to me. You had too much schoolwork to see Milt's son, but you had time for this boy."

"For God's sake, Dad, I'm twenty-two and I can pick my own boyfriends."

Jack paced to the loveseat in the living room area and sat down. "Yes, you're twenty-two, but I'm still paying the bills, and you know the kind of boy I think is appropriate for you."

"Yeah, Josh Goodman, who's, by the way, a complete asshole," she said and paused for a moment, sat down in an armchair across from her father and tried to gather as much courage as she could. She hated these battles with her father. It always ended with her conceding to his wishes, but doing exactly what she wanted to do discreetly. He had no right to interfere with her love life, money or no money.

Jack leaned forward and shouted. "How could you? How could you like that boy?"

Rebecca matched his volume. "Why? Because he's not Jewish? Because he's German?"

"He looks like a biker, for God's sake."

"And, if he was dressed in a Brooks Brother's suit, would that make a difference?"

Jack paused for a moment and stood up. "I could use a drink. What do you have?"

"A drink is not going to change anything."

He glared at her until she gave in.

"I have the pinot noir you brought the last time you were here."

"Fine," he said and went over to the kitchen alcove, opened the cabinet, removed the bottle and a glass and filled it to the top. He swigged down half of it, stepped over to the loveseat carefully and sat down. God forbid he should spill a drop.

"Do you think it was easy for me? Mother and father, both Holocaust survivors and both so paranoid, always looking over their shoulders, afraid that something awful was going to happen to them again. The never-ending nightmares, the screams, night after night after night," he said in a soft, measured voice. "My father, so beaten down and so guarded, like a turtle who only pops his head out of his shell every once in a while, mostly to eat," he said, draining his glass of wine. "And my mother was extremely over-protective. You think I'm over-protective? You have no idea. She was like a mother grizzly bear defending her last surviving cub. And if I was late, even only for fifteen minutes, if I didn't call, she'd call the police and have the whole neighborhood searching for me. I felt so suffocated and yet I didn't ever want to do anything that would hurt them. They suffered enough for one lifetime." Tears welled up in his eyes. "Do you think I could forget that and say well, it's all in the past?"

Rebecca absorbed her father's words. He'd never talked about his childhood before, and she'd never seen him on the verge of tears. Never. Even when her mother was dying of cancer, her father always maintained his stoic demeanor.

She had thought that her father's childhood must have been difficult, but she had no idea the effect it had on his life. She moved to edge of her chair and bent forward.

"I'm not saying you should forget. But, Daddy, Kurt is not a Nazi. His parents weren't even born yet."

"No, Kurt is not a Nazi and his parents weren't Nazis. But his grandparents could have been."

Rebecca studied her father's face. The wrinkles under his eyes, the tightness of the skin around his lips, his thinning hair, made him appear harder and more uncompromising than usual.

"And what does hating all Germans make you?"

"I don't care what it makes me. I have a right to the way I feel and I don't hate all Germans. I drive a Mercedes, for God's sake, and go to Berlin frequently. I have business and friends there. I just don't want my only child to be romantically involved with one."

"Grandma was the one who was in Auschwitz, not you. She's gotten to know Kurt and is very fond of him. She told you so herself." She walked over to the wine bottle on her counter and poured herself a glass.

"Your grandmother was the one who called me a couple of

months ago. She was very concerned and upset about you and Kurt. That's why I'm here now. That's why I pushed up my trip."

"Yes, I know, but she called you before we even started dating. She's very fond of him now. They've become friends."

Jack stood up, went over to the kitchen counter, poured himself another glass of wine and moved slowly toward her.

"Rebecca, you're my only child and you know how much I love you. But, I'm telling you, I want you to stop seeing this boy immediately and that's final."

She rose, faced her father, fixing her eyes directly on his face. "You can't tell me to do this. You can't."

Chapter 35

While the sun disappeared into the horizon, a steady stream of joggers whizzed by Rebecca and Kurt as they leaned against the railing overlooking the East River, just as they did months ago: the same time and place of their first date.

Tears trickled down Rebecca's face. "I just won't listen to him. I'm not going to stop seeing you. We'll just have to be more careful," she said staring into his wet eyes, but all she could see was her father's tense face, his forbidding words bursting out of his mouth.

Kurt turned her toward him and held her tightly. She snuggled her face to his chest. "Christ, Rebecca, we've been careful. Should we walk around wearing disguises? You have four years of medical school. Do you really want to give that up? You need him now." He took her hand in his. "I asked your grandmother if she would talk to him for us. She didn't say yes, but she didn't say no either. Maybe she'll help."

"I'm not sure it would make any difference," she said, knowing it would be impossible to change her father's mind. Both judge and jury, he made the decision she knew he would make if he found out about Kurt.

She kissed him again heatedly as if it was for the last time.

*   *   *

Rebecca's beautiful face streaked with tears haunted Kurt as he approached the Y. He barely had enough strength to open the door. He made his way toward the elevators, drowning in self-pity. Just when he was becoming optimistic about his life, everything once again seemed bleak. He felt cursed, as if someone had a Kurt Lichter voodoo doll and was sticking pin after pin in it.

"Hey, Romeo . . ."

Kurt gaped at Tony struggling with a guitar case and a large amp, heading toward him. Kurt didn't answer. He was in no mood to deal with Tony's schtick.

Tony raised his voice, commanding Kurt's attention. "O Romeo, Romeo, wherefore art thou, Romeo?"

"What's up?" he said, surrendering.

"Can you give me a hand with this shit? The fucking bass player's car broke down so I've got to lug all this via subway."

Kurt grabbed the guitar from Tony. "Where to?"

"Would you believe, Queens?"

"Queens? Where's that?"

"You've never been to Queens? My friend, you can't say you live in New York City unless you've been to at least one of its outer boroughs."

"Okay. Why the fuck not?" he said, welcoming the distraction. What else did he have to do?

They trudged toward the Lexington Avenue subway. Kurt helped Tony carry the amp down the subway steps with one hand, while holding the guitar with the other. They struggled through the turnstile and raced to the awaiting train as the doors were closing. Tony stuck his foot in the subway door just in time. They rushed inside, luckily found seats, and collapsed into them.

For the next thirty minutes Kurt poured his heart out to his only friend, telling him the continuing saga of what he called his life. Tony listened quietly and Kurt began to wonder if should be telling him any of this. Clearly he wouldn't be much help. But it felt good to let it out and to get out of the city. With each subway stop he felt a little bit lighter.

Kurt and Tony descended from the Sunnyside, Queens, Fortieth Street stop on the elevated IRT Flushing line. They made their way down the steep steps lugging the guitar and amp onto Queens Boulevard.

The area reminded him of some districts in Berlin with its old brick two-, three- and six-story buildings, small shops and neighborhood bars.

"So this is Queens, very provincial, not at all like Manhattan," Kurt said. "It's similar to the district where I grew up."

"Come, we still have to walk a couple of blocks before we reach our destination, O'Reilly's Pub. This district is called Sunnyside. It's home to mostly working class folks and a lot of twenty-somethings as the rent is much cheaper than in the city. Also my favorite piece of trivia about Sunnyside is that The Ramones played some of their earliest gigs in the pubs here."

"Really? 'I Want to be Sedated' is still one of my favorite songs. In fact, one of the original members, Douglas Colvin, aka Dee Dee Ramone, came from Germany. They were and still are very popular in Berlin. There's even a Ramones Museum inside a bar."

"Yeah, I heard about that. You can take me there when you get kicked back to Berlin."

"Thanks for your vote of confidence," Kurt said as they passed a storefront art gallery. He backtracked and peeked inside the window and saw a beautiful abstract piece that resembled stained glass with intersecting bold colors—purple, orange and red—and contemporary landscapes done with muted colors, barely visible representations of lakes and trees. He was mesmerized by these images, and ideas began jumping around in his head for paintings, as often happened when he thought of himself as an artist.

"Hey, Michelangelo, we got to get moving, it's just at the end of the block," Tony said and pulled him away from the window. They stopped in front of O'Reilly's Pub. Tony pointed to a sign posted in the window: THE TOAD BOYS, PLAYING TONIGHT

"The Toad Boys?" Kurt grinned. "Cool name."

"I'm not officially in the band, just pitching in for a friend. A gig's a gig, right?"

"Absolutely."

"Anyway, this place is one of the hottest pubs in this neighborhood because it has live music every weekend. Last year, the owner's son finally convinced his dad to let him bring in bands on Friday and Saturday nights to increase revenue, and it worked."

Tony and Kurt dragged the amp into the bar. Kurt glanced around the pub which was packed with a mixture of what Kurt thought might be blue-collar locals with their outdated tee shirts and baseball caps, and young Manhattanites, dressed in trendy tee shirts and designer jeans, who were drawn there by lower priced beers and entertainment with no cover charge. The long bar was black with red vinyl barstools, all occupied.

"Give me a hand with this, please," Tony said.

Kurt helped load Tony's amp onto a small raised platform, while the other players were setting up their amps and instruments. He was grateful that this part of the job was done for now, at least until the show was over. Tony introduced Kurt to the other members of the band, all carbon copies of Tony: lean, long hair, dressed in tight jeans and black tee shirts, not unlike Kurt's attire and general appearance. If The Toad Boys needed another retro punky guy on stage, he would fit in perfectly.

Tony pointed to a dark wooden table to the right of the bandstand with a large pitcher of beer and mugs in the middle.

"And, Kurt, thanks, you can sit at that table over there. It's reserved for the band and their guests. Help yourself to the beer, you earned it."

Kurt jumped off the so-called stage as the band began their set, covering the heavy metal hits of Metallica, Guns and Roses, and Pearl Jam. It was loud and repetitive—a deadly combination. He poured himself a mug, guzzled the bland tasting American beer while he watched Tony struggle with the tempo on the first song and empathized with him. It was apparent that he was new to the band. By the third song, Tony played in tempo, but it was clear that the Toad Boys were not thrilled with their replacement. After lugging all that shit to Queens, it seemed hardly worth it. Yet, his friend was the most committed person he'd ever known when it came to his music. He admired Tony's tenacity. Practicing every day and night, performing at jam sessions all over the city whenever he could, he was totally devoted to becoming the best guitar player he could possibly be.

Sitting alone at the table he could not stop his mind from wandering back to Rebecca's kiss, and was fearful that he'd never see her again. He'd tossed down several mugs of beer by the time the band finished their first set. Loud, recorded music took over where the live music left off. The other members of the band headed directly to the bar to mingle with the patrons without saying a word to Tony, obviously shunning him.

"Sorry, man," Kurt said as Tony sat down next to him.

"It's okay. It be that way sometimes when you're filling in for someone the last minute. I never had even one rehearsal with this fucking band. But thanks anyway for bailing me out."

Tony noticed the half-empty pitcher of beer and stared at Kurt. "And I'm sorry about you and Rebecca," he said, pouring himself a mug. "Dude, when my father wanted to marry my mother, his Jewish parents went ballistic. Their only son, marrying a Catholic girl."

"Ah, a *shiksa*," Kurt added.

"Yep and his mother threatened to stick her head in the oven. His father threatened to cut him out of his will. Some serious shit went down."

So he had been listening. Typical Tony, listens, digest it, then when you least expect it, lays it all out for you.

"What happened?" Kurt asked.

"My dad stood his ground. He didn't budge an inch. It was true love. Hard to believe knowing the two of them," he said, gulping down the last of his beer. "Anyway, my dad's parents eventually came around. In the end, they didn't want to lose their only son."

"And your mother and father lived happily ever after," Kurt said, encouraged.

"Not exactly. They got divorced three years ago. They lasted twenty-five miserable years, but most likely, they would've been unhappy with anyone they married. My point is that you worry too much. You never know what people will do. All I'm saying is that it's not over until it's over," he said, punctuating his last sentence by pounding the table with his mug. Noticing that the Toad Boys were returning to the stage for the second set, he jumped up and joined them.

By the fifth song, he was given a nod by the lead singer to take the legendary solo riff in the classic Steely Dan song and his fingers hammered it out with ease. Tony's face gleamed with confidence as he bowed his head to the audience in appreciation of their resounding applause. At least this night wasn't a total loss.

Kurt emptied what was left of the beer, wondering what disastrous event awaited him. He had always chosen the rockiest road possible to follow. Depression and misery were his constant companions. Even as a child he was more comfortable being disappointed than pleased. Was he drawn to Rebecca because he knew it would turn out badly? Maybe Karin was right; maybe he didn't know how to do "happy."

Chapter 36

Kurt entered the Jewish Seniors Office, fearing and expecting the worst. David's voice sounded as somber as it did when he was summoned by him to have a "talk" after his shouting match with Sadie. He couldn't imagine what he'd done this time. He approached David's desk with trepidation and viewed the grave expression on his face. The only other time Kurt saw that expression was when the synagogue had been vandalized.

David stood up and ushered him into the conference room. He pulled the desk chair from behind the desk and gestured to turn the chair in front of the desk so that the two chairs were facing each other. Kurt did so and sat down.

"What is it with you? Trouble seems to find you, no matter what. Everybody wants to send you back to Germany."

"Who . . . who now?"

"Mrs. Seidenberg's son, Jack was just here. He was extremely agitated. He wants you out of the country and if possible off the planet, ASAP."

"Can he do that?"

"It's possible. Jack Seidenberg is a big *macher* attorney in L.A., with powerful connections here in New York. He knows some very influential people from The Federation of Jewish Philanthropies, who help fund us, and is a good friend of ex-Mayor Bloomberg."

"I never even met Mr. Seidenberg. Why is he treating me like I'm a wanted criminal?"

David leaned toward him. "You're seeing his daughter and that's breaking his law."

"I've done everything you told me to do. I changed. You even said so yourself. You called me a *mensch* and that's a good thing. Right? I worked the hardest I've ever worked in my life. I helped restore the synagogue and I made peace with Mrs. Seidenberg. We're even friends now—good friends. You know that," Kurt said.

"Yes, you and Sadie are good friends now, but according to Jack Seidenberg, his mother is the reason he pushed up his trip to New York in the first place. She called her son and warned him about you and Rebecca before the synagogue's restoration, back when you and Sadie were sparring partners, before you transformed from being a hostile, angry young man into a *mensch*, remember?"

"Yes, yes, I know this and I know all about Rebecca's father. But I asked Sadie to help, to talk to her son now, and make him change his mind about me. Why hasn't she done this already?"

"I don't have the answer to that, you'll have to ask her," David said and placed his hand gently on Kurt's shoulder. "Maybe I can figure something out. In the meantime, please stay away from his daughter. Okay? Will you do that?"

Kurt turned red with rage. Why does everything in life always turn to shit. His body temperature rose so rapidly, he felt as if he was about to burst into flames.

*   *   *

Kurt stomped down the street and passed the clean, refreshed synagogue, which seemed to only fuel his fire. He approached the projects and viewed the usual gang of kids hanging out in front of the entrance to Sadie's building. They took one look at Kurt's face and scattered.

As Kurt pushed the door open, Leon was about to exit and waited for Kurt to come in. "Young man, I loved your drawing of Sadie and her granddaughter. I just helped her hang it in her living room. What an amazing portrait. You can see the likeness between them, particularly in the eyes and in their smiles. You have no idea how proud she is of you," Leon said, shaking Kurt's hand.

Kurt shrugged his shoulders dismissively and trudged to the elevator. All he could think of was being banished back to Germany like he was a known terrorist. He boarded and pounded on the number six button as if it were cursed. He searched for the right words that would convince Sadie to make her son rescind his threats against him.

The elevator stopped and Kurt forged his way to Sadie's door. He thought of banging on the door, but decided to knock a few times instead. He didn't really want to frighten her. He heard Sadie's fracture boot pounding on the floor.

"Who's there?"

"Kurt . . . Kurt Lichter," he said, emphasizing his last name.

Sadie opened the door, led Kurt into the living room and gestured for him to sit on the couch. She refrained from looking at his outraged face, averting his defiant stare.

"Can I get you something? A glass of juice, water, some tea, a piece of fruit?"

"No, no. I don't want anything. I didn't come for a social visit."

"I know, I know why you're here." She sat in her chair and rested her hands on the armrests, as if bracing herself.

Kurt spotted his drawing mounted on the wall across from the couch and felt a brief wave of satisfaction seeing it displayed so prominently.

"How could you?" he said, inadvertently raising his voice. "We confided in each other, we became good friends. Why didn't you call your son after the synagogue and tell him not to come?"

"I was going to, but he already made his plans. I thought when he got here I could smooth things over. I tried, believe me, I tried. I was wrong, I couldn't change his mind about you. I'm so sorry."

He gazed at her face, swathed in sorrow and shame, but continued grilling her. "Did you know he met with David? Do you know what he wants to do to me now?"

Sadie bowed her head. "I know he's forbidden Rebecca to see you."

Kurt's eyes burned with rage. "Not only that, he wants to have me thrown out of this country. He wants me shipped back to Berlin like I was damaged goods."

"Oh my God. I didn't know he spoke to David. He didn't tell me that. I had no idea he would do something that harsh. He's my only child, but the way he is now, he's like a stranger to me. I know I wasn't the best mother . . . those years were so difficult for me, my memories plagued me night and day."

She rose from her chair, crossed to the couch and sat next to Kurt. "I want to tell you something. Please let me . . ."

Kurt wanted to hear her explanation, that's why he was there, but was conflicted by his fondness and his hatred of her at the moment. He felt like he had a stick of dynamite in his brain with its fuse nearing the final blast. He placed his hand on her arm and nodded.

"I've always tried to be a fair and open person, even after all I went through during the war. That was a very, very long time ago and I didn't really think about it—a young, German man, in my house. I thought it was a wonderful idea in theory and I agreed to it, but when you came that first time and I saw you there with your blue eyes, blond hair, your thick, German accent, your high black leather boots, you looked like one of them, you sounded like one of them, even with the earring and the motorcycle jacket. Something happened to me. It was like you brought back all of those years that were hidden, buried down deep. It was like a flood raging inside of me, all that fear, hate, pain, shame and guilt. Oh my God, the guilt."

"Guilt? You? You were the victim."

"Yes, yes, me."

"I've heard of survivor's guilt from my orientation at Project Remembrance and David. They said that Holocaust survivors feel guilty for being alive while their loved ones were all murdered, but I didn't fully understand it. I still don't. Why would you feel guilty? What could you have done against the power of the Nazis?"

Sadie stood up and stepped past him. "Come, come follow me. I want to show you something."

Kurt followed her into the bedroom; she opened the closet door and pointed to a shelf above her. "See, up there, the old portfolio, could you take it down, please."

He reached for an aged, large, brown, expanding folder, tied with threadbare string. As he held it, he knew that the contents of this folder were extremely significant.

"Please go ahead and put it on the bed," she said, gaping at the folder as if it were Pandora's Box and something horrible would burst out of it at any moment. Kurt placed it on the bed with caution and moved it toward her.

"You open it. Take them out. I've never showed them to anyone before, not even my Max, may he rest in peace, but I want you to see them," she said, her face fraught with anguish.

Kurt unfastened the string, lifted up the flap, expanded the folder and peered into it. He viewed bits and pieces of paper, yellowed and frayed with age. He was afraid to touch them, fearful that if he breathed on them too heavily, they would disintegrate.

She patted his arm. "Go ahead, lay them on the bed."

Kurt removed the fragile scraps of paper, arranged them on the bed, gasping at the horrific images before him: ashen, tormented, gaunt faces, laden with terror. He was both repelled and mesmerized by these drawings. Sadie turned her head away; she could not bear to look at them.

"Oh my God, Mrs. Seidenberg, are these yours, I mean did you draw these?" he asked. Sadie nodded. "When you were in . . ."

"In the camp. Yes, in Auschwitz. I haven't looked at them since the end of the war. I haven't had the heart."

"The Nazis let you draw them? They gave you the paper and pencils?"

Sadie pointed to the chair beside the bed. "Sit down."

He dropped into the chair. Sadie sat on the edge of the bed and leaned into him.

"A short time after we were shipped to the camp, they put me to work washing the sheets and towels for the S.S. If you were young and strong, they kept you alive . . . barely alive. Otherwise, they gassed you to death upon arrival. I found a scrap of paper in the garbage bin in the laundry room. I quickly snatched it up and hid it in my panties. I thought that maybe I could draw something on it. I missed drawing so much. Later in the barracks, I took out the crumpled paper, pressed it out with both hands as best as I could."

Sadie got up and walked around the bed and picked up one of the drawings and stared at it. "A young woman, I hardly knew in Berlin, we called her Gerty, short for Gertrude. She was so emaciated, you could count the number of bones in her ribcage, so very different than the statuesque beautiful girl with long, dark hair and green eyes I remembered before the Nazis."

Sadie bent over the bed and showed the drawing to Kurt. He flinched when he looked at the horrifying rendering of a cadaverous woman, scarcely alive.

"My mother fitted her wedding gown and Gerty remembered my drawing of her. She had an old chewed up pencil. I never asked where she got it. She begged me to draw her . . . to document what had become of her in the camp. I squatted down, used the wooden floor as an easel and laid the piece of paper in front of me. Everyone in the barracks gathered around and watched as I sketched Gerty's skeletal face. Oh my God, that face, it haunted my nightmares after the war."

Sadie placed the drawing back down on the bed and walked around back to her place on the bed, across from Kurt and continued her story.

"When I was almost finished, a guard barged in. He was in his late twenties, stocky, with a shock of yellow hair worn straight across his forehead and a small blond mustache, Adolph Hitler style. His name was Sergeant Fuchs, and he caught me sketching Gerty. Maybe, one of the woman guards, who would from time to time peek through the windows of our barracks to check up on us, spotted me drawing. Any artistic activity was a punishable offense. He crouched down and plucked the paper from the floor and studied it. He cocked his head from side to side as if he was an art critic. He then neatly folded it and put it in his pocket and left. The next morning he singled me out at roll call. I remember that cold, dark morning like it was yesterday. Thousands of prisoners lined up consuming every available inch of space in the prison yard with Nazi guards swarming over them like angry bees. Sergeant Fuchs grabbed me off the line. I thought he was going to shoot me right there on the spot, but instead he presented me to General Eberhardt, who was about forty-five, heavy-set with a huge pot belly that made the buttons on his uniform pop out as if they were magically suspended from the button holes. Fuchs told Eberhardt that I was an excellent artist even though I was only seventeen and that I was just as good as the other camp artists, whose work was displayed in the camp's art museum. He pulled my drawing of Gerty from his pocket, unfolded it and showed it to the General, who was very pleased. He said that he thought my talent would impress the Commandant of the camp and ordered me to do his portrait."

Kurt hung on every word Sadie uttered, leaned forward and sat on the edge of the chair. "There was an art museum in Auschwitz?"

"Yes. The commandant at the time, *Obersturmbannführer* Rudolf Höss, started an art museum at the behest of one of the inmates, Franciszak Targosz, who was a Polish artist, convincing Höss that it would bring culture to the Nazi officers stationed there and to impress visiting Nazi dignitaries. But, only the Polish artists could have their work displayed in the museum. There was also an eighty-piece orchestra comprised of prisoners, the finest musicians in Europe before the war. The Nazis had endless ways of exploiting the talents of their captives."

"Did you draw the general's portrait?"

"Yes. He gave me a large sketch pad, charcoal sticks and pens. I was so frightened, my hands shook. If he didn't like it, he could have had me beaten or executed in a blink of an eye. He was not easy to draw. He had a gap between his two upper center front teeth and had one of those faces that resisted a close shave; a faint stubble always remained under his nose and chin. I was smart, much smarter than I am now, so I made him look more handsome than he was and he loved the portrait. I became his new protégé. I was very busy after that. I no longer worked in the laundry. I did family portraits, portraits of high ranking Nazi officials, instruction manuals, even Christmas cards. They had never ending uses for my talent. In return, I got a little more food than the others, who were all starving to death, and General Eberhardt even arranged for my sister, Esther, to live with me in my barracks."

Sadie paused for a moment, her eyes narrowed, her face tightened, she took a deep breath and continued. "Esther worked on the cleaning detail at the time, and every day she would smuggle all kinds of forms: clerical papers, work orders, Nazi stationary, whatever she could steal, and brought them back to me so I could draw on the back of them. Even though I was officially a camp artist, I was forbidden to draw on my own. I sketched all the women in my barracks. They had been reduced to skin and bones, sickly, soiled, weak bodies, as if the blood or any signs of life had been drained out of them. Half of them were dying of typhus. Night after night, I would grab the pilfered pencils and pens from under my mattress. Esther said it was important that we record what had become of us, to provide evidence, to show the world . . ."

She put her hand on her chest. "Maybe I should stop now. I'm telling you too much. How much more can the both of us take? My heart is ready to explode," she said, gazing at Kurt's mesmerized face.

"No, no, please go on. I want to hear the rest of your story. I want to understand," he pleaded.

"I just wanted to draw and I needed to keep my sister and myself alive. That was all I wished for. Then one day when Esther left her work detail, some forms fell out of her skirt. She picked them up immediately and jammed them back into her underpants. She hurried back to barracks, told me about what happened and swore that nobody saw her. I always begged her to be careful. A little while after, a guard I'd never seen before, who was blond, lean and tall stormed in and pointed his rifle at Esther. He had frightening, piercing blue eyes with a gray tinge . . ."

"Like mine?" Kurt asked, clutching Sadie's hand, his voice quivering.

Sadie nodded. "I'm sorry to say that you bear an uncanny resemblance to him, which is where all the trouble with Jack began. Anyway, I stood there frozen. I was so mortified. He first ordered Esther to lift up her skirt. He peered at her panties and lowered his rifle toward them. He commanded her to remove the papers. She did and all of the smuggled forms fell to the floor. Somehow, she remained calm. She was so fearless, so courageous, *Esther mayn shvester*; she didn't even bat an eye. My heart dropped to my knees. My whole body shook. He then shouted at her to take off her blouse. She removed it and several pencils tumbled out. He raised his gun, aimed it at her head, cocked the barrel, yelling '*Gelegenheitsdieb*' over and over again and pulled the trigger," Sadie said, holding onto the edge of the bed for support. "The air reeked with the smell of gun powder. I could hardly catch my breath. Esther plummeted to the floor, lifeless. I cried out, the guard quickly turned his rifle and aimed it at my heart, but he didn't pull the trigger. He just did an about face and marched off. I'll never know why he didn't kill me, too. Maybe he knew that witnessing my little sister's murder right in front of me was worse than killing me. He left the barracks with my dear, beautiful Esther lying half-naked and dead before me." She faced Kurt, trembling. "He killed my sweet, brave Esther. Here. Let me show you her picture."

She stood up, went around the bed and surveyed all the faces staring back at her. Kurt followed. She picked one up, fixed her eyes on it for a moment and then handed it to him.

Kurt held it with both hands, aware of its fragility and importance. He studied the image of the young fragile, noble girl with short chopped hair, almond shaped eyes and a small pointed nose. "And I did nothing," Sadie cried. "She was stealing paper and pencils for me and I stood there and did nothing."

"What could you do? You were young yourself. What could you have done? He would have shot you, too," he said, wiping away his tears with the back of his hand.

"First my mother, most likely my father and brother, and then my sister. I would wake up in the dead of night, screaming, why me? Why am I still here and everyone else I loved is dead?"

Kurt carefully placed the picture of Esther back on the bed and wrapped his arms around Sadie. "You can't blame yourself, Mrs. Seidenberg."

She pulled away from him, calmly. "After the liberation, I couldn't even look at a sheet of paper, or think about drawing again without shaking. I just couldn't. Not until the synagogue. Not until Moses—with you."

She touched his arm gently. "I guess I couldn't stop forever."

He took her hand in his. "Once an artist, always an artist . . . I am so, so very, very sorry . . . I can't tell you how sorry I am."

"Look at you. You're paying back a debt you don't even owe."

"It was Germans, my ancestors, who robbed you of your family, who stole your life from you when you should have been going to university studying art. I feel like it's my debt and I'm happy to honor it."

Sadie nodded and Kurt longed to see her smile once more. It had been such a pleasure, just a short while ago, when she had flung the door open and welcomed him with open arms. He would do whatever it took to make sure that Sadie Seidenberg smiled again. But apparently, Sadie had something else in mind.

Chapter 37

A yellow cab pulled up in front of the Plaza Hotel. Kurt hopped out first, again in Tony's suit, a gray wool scarf draped around his neck that Sadie gave him and insisted he wear for extra warmth.

He assisted Sadie, who was bundled up in her down coat, out onto the curb. A cheery, rosy cheeked doorman raced to the cab door and held it open for them as they entered the luxurious lobby with its marble floors, crystal chandeliers and old world style Louis XIV furnishings.

Kurt examined the lobby as they headed with their arms linked toward the elevators. "Beautiful hotel, very European. It is similar to the Hotel Adlon Kempinski in Berlin."

"Fancy, schmancy. I should have worn my ball gown."

They reached the bank of elevators and found one waiting for them. The operator slid the gate open, welcomed them in, and Sadie informed him that they were going to the fifteenth floor. Kurt noticed the elevator had a floor to ceiling mirror on the back wall and did a last-minute check of his appearance. He straightened his tie, brushed any lingering remains of lint off of Tony's suit and ran his fingers through his hair, ensuring that there were no stray locks to alter his slicked back hairstyle.

Sadie patted his arm, smiling. "You look like a perfect gentleman and very handsome. Stop worrying."

The elevator reached the fifteenth floor. Sadie thanked the operator, linked her arm through Kurt's, and they stepped out into the hallway. Kurt checked the room direction sign, steering Sadie to the right.

They reached their desired destination, Room 1519. Sadie knocked on the door, and a booming male voice streamed into the hallway, the same commanding voice that he had heard at Rebecca's apartment a few weeks ago.

"Damn bellboy, I told him to come in a half-hour. Would you get the door, please?"

Anxiety surged within Kurt, hearing that demanding tone again.

Rebecca opened the door and gasped at the sight of the visitors. "Grandma, Kurt, what are you doing here?"

Kurt registered Rebecca's shocked expression and was surprised himself as he had no idea that she would be there. He wondered if Sadie knew and had deliberately kept it from him. But why?

He decided to remain silent and allow Sadie to take the lead, as this visit was her idea. He was glad Rebecca was there as an additional layer of support. He didn't think it would work, but Sadie said it was the only way. She had to try harder to change Jack's mind.

"Rebecca, who's there?" Jack called out.

"We were in the neighborhood and thought we'd drop by. Aren't you going to invite us in?" Sadie said with a sly grin and Rebecca reluctantly ushered them in.

Kurt surveyed the large suite. It was decorated in the same French provincial style as in the lobby; the citrus scent of men's cologne infused the air. He stared at his nemesis, Jack Seidenberg, taking in his flared nostrils and fuming eyes.

Sadie moved toward her son, leading Kurt by the hand. "Jack, I want you to meet my friend, Kurt Lichter . . ."

Jack stepped backward. "I should have known. Always meddling."

"Hear the boy out, that's all I ask," Sadie said.

"Stay out of this, Mom, it's none of your business."

"You're my son, Rebecca is my granddaughter, and Kurt is my friend. It's most definitely my business."

Kurt decided to intervene on his own behalf and took a step toward Jack. "Please Mr. Seidenberg, please give me a chance to—"

"Why? Why should I give you a chance?" Jack shouted.

"Do it for me," Sadie said, placing her hand on her tenacious son's shoulder.

Fearfully, Kurt watched Sadie and Jack spar back and forth. He had no idea what his fate was going to be.

Rebecca moved toward her father. "Daddy, can't you at least listen to him?"

Kurt found it hard to believe how obstinate Jack was being. His own mother and daughter pleading with him to be reasonable and he would not budge. Just as he thought. Jack reminded him of his own father, who would have reacted in the same way if he was cornered like this. His stance, the way he stood with his chest pressed out and his feet a foot apart, ready to take on any opponents that would challenge him was comparable.

Suddenly, defying all logic, Jack turned to Kurt. "Okay, okay, what is it you want from me?"

Ah yes, Kurt thought, lawyers are trained to listen to the opposing argument. His professional training had gotten the better of him.

Kurt was silent for a moment, then picked his words carefully.

"I don't want to cause you any trouble, believe me, Mr. Seidenberg," he said and gazed at Rebecca for a moment as she rooted him on with her eyes, bolstering his courage. "I care very much for your daughter and your mother. They are both amazing women. I would like to be able to finish out my term here and continue to see Rebecca with your blessing."

Jack averted his eyes from Kurt's gaze. "I was raised by two Holocaust survivors and I have been living in the shadow of it my whole life and you, a German descendant, are asking me to just bury the past and for permission to have a relationship with my only child?"

"I am not asking you to forget the past or for forgiveness," Kurt countered. "I know that what happened is unforgivable."

Sadie moved in front of Kurt and seized her son's hand. "Jack, for God's sake, I'm telling you this is a good boy."

Jack pushed Sadie's hand off his. "How could you of all people—after all you've been through—be on his side?"

"Jack, you're my son, my only child, and you think I'm against you? I know this is my fault, you being the way you are. I know it must have been very difficult for you growing up with me and your father, both of us so terribly scarred. I really couldn't handle being a mother at that time. It's the reason why we waited to have children and why we never had another child. I just don't want you to harm an innocent boy and make life miserable for Rebecca."

Kurt gazed at Sadie's pleading face and observed Jack's stern posture, his unshakable presence.

"I know what's best for my own daughter," Jack roared.

Kurt turned his gaze toward Rebecca, who was transfixed on her father's face.

"No you don't. Do you really think making trouble for Kurt with his organization, getting him kicked out of the country, and taking me away from someone I truly care about is what's best for me?"

Unable to contain himself, Kurt moved next to Rebecca and

faced Jack. "Judge me for who I am now and for who I am working so hard to become in the future. Please don't judge me just because of my ancestry and where I was born."

"Okay, okay, I've heard enough." Jack threw his hands up in the air, his face flushed with anger.

Kurt could feel Jack's deeply rooted conflict, how hard he was holding onto his outdated beliefs and almost felt sorry for him.

The doorbell rang, visibly jarring everyone in the room as if they were in a boxing ring and the bell unexpectedly signaled the end of the first round seconds after it had started.

"That must be the bellboy," Jack said and hurried to answer the door. Wheeling a luggage cart, the bellboy entered and loaded Jack's bags while everyone in the room watched him with expressionless faces, as though they were in a state of shock.

Kurt, Rebecca and Sadie trailed behind Jack as he briskly exited the hotel behind the bellboy and they looked on silently as he loaded Jack's luggage into the trunk of a waiting limousine.

Jack stepped toward the passenger door and turned around and faced them. He slowly shifted his gaze from one to the other.

Sadie walked forward. "You know, Jack, a wise man remembers the past and takes responsibility for it, but isn't controlled by it. He doesn't let it cloud the present or destroy the future."

Jack stared at his mother with disdain. "And who said that?"

"I just did, who else?" she said, ignoring his contempt.

Jack and Kurt looked at each other, seemingly one waiting for the other to make the first move. Kurt extended his hand toward his worthy adversary. Jack waited for a moment and shook it briefly and limply, as if he were doing it for show. His heart wasn't in it.

"I'll talk to David and tell him to cease and desist," Jack the lawyer finally conceded and Kurt could see the Jewish warrior crumbling. This might be the first time in his life he surrendered, and it showed.

Rebecca gave her father a kiss on his cheek. He hugged her tightly.

"This is the hardest thing I've ever done," he said.

"I know, letting go is never easy."

Sadie then took her turn hugging him. "I'm proud of you, son."

Jack nodded and got into the limo. It swiftly merged into traffic. Kurt took Rebecca's hand and put his arm around Sadie, as the unlikely threesome stood and watched the limo heading down Park Avenue.

A great sense of relief washed over Kurt. It was hard to believe he won this battle, but for the first time in his life things didn't turn to shit. On the contrary, he would finish out his term with Project Remembrance, continue to see Rebecca and Sadie, and maybe instead of painting his nightmares he would find new subjects to capture. He felt as if he had just received a pardon for a crime he didn't commit.

Only six months ago, wandering the streets of Berlin accompanied by his own anger and despair, his one salvation was Karin and the hope that he would somehow reunite with her in New York and take a bite out of America's Big Apple. His only option to leave Berlin was to join Project Remembrance, a peace group formed to atone for the sins of the Nazis, which at the time he thought pathetic and couldn't care less about.

He thought about how defensive he felt about the Holocaust during his school years. Not every German was a Nazi. Not every German participated in mass murder. He was taught about *Widerstand,* the German resistance to Nazism. There were thousands of Germans killed for their involvement in that movement. His teacher spent more time on the failed attempts to overthrow Hitler than the extermination of six million Jews, plus thousands of Gypsies and homosexuals. He even wrote a report for his history class about Claus Von Stauffenberg who engineered Valkyrie, the largest plot to kill Hitler in 1944, and was tempted to bring that up to Rebecca whenever they talked about the Holocaust. Fortunately, his sixth sense stopped him. He knew that those failed attempts by a small percentage of Germans would not be accepted by her as any kind of vindication.

Yet, somehow, Hannah Kruger of that organization thought he was good enough to send to New York to work with Jewish seniors and even though at the beginning he tried his best to prove her wrong, he ended up surprising himself by proving her right.

Rebecca snuggled her head on his shoulder, her lavender scent swirling all about him as Jack's limo faded out of sight. "Well, what shall we do now?"

"I don't know about you two, but I'm starving. Negotiating with a hotshot lawyer sure works up an appetite," Sadie said.

"I know a great kosher restaurant downtown that David took me to a few months ago, but I can't remember the name," Kurt said.

Sadie removed her arm from Kurt's back and linked her arm through his. "You mean, Noah's Ark—they have the best matzah ball soup in New York. I love that place."

"Yeah, that's it."

"I've been meaning to check it out," Rebecca said.

Kurt stepped forward to hail a cab. "Something tells me I'll enjoy it more with you guys than I did with David."

A taxi with screeching brakes swerved toward the curb and stopped an inch in front of them. Kurt assisted Sadie into the cab, and Rebecca slid in next to her. Kurt got in and closed the door, and as the bright yellow taxi merged with the heaving, honking New York traffic, Rebecca took his hand. The warmth of her hand in his counteracted the cold wind on his cheeks and for the first time in his life he felt blessed. He stroked her hair and at last understood that concept. It had always been alien to him. What the fuck would he feel blessed about? He now had found a reason to feel happy and whole and he promised himself and a God he'd only recently started to think might exist, that he would hang onto that feeling forever.

Ronnie Berman is the author of her debut novel *Drawing From Memory*. She has studied novel writing at UCLA Extension. A former screenwriter she has had three of her screenplays optioned. She has also placed twice as a semi-finalist in the Chesterfield Foundation competition and placed twice as a semi-finalist in the Writers Foundation America's Best Competition. She holds an M.A. in Arts in Education from New York University. Her first career in Education was teaching kindergarten in the New York City public school system and her last career was in computer programming, In between she traveled around Europe by herself for a year and worked as a bartender in a busy London pub and tutored English in the Canary Islands, epitomizing the diverse experiences she has had in her life.

Author Berman is currently living in Los Angeles, CA with her husband Bob Maslen and for fun she volunteers once a week reading stories to children at her local library.

Made in the USA
Las Vegas, NV
25 January 2022

42362701R00135